JESUS LOVES YOUR HISTORY

ASHLIE S. CHRISTIE

"No matter who you are, where you come from, how you go about changing... Jesus loves who you were, who you are, and who you are becoming. Be gentle with yourself and others... you never know who you are talking to, as God is within us all."

-Ash

Previous Working Titles:

A Book.

Noah & Hank.

Forgiveness Meetings.

The Personal Steps.

Jesus Loves Your History LLC

2nd Edition 2022.

1st Edition 2014.

Copyright ©2014-2022 by Ashlie s. Christie [USA & Ireland]

Edited By: Doris Foster [Nigeria]

Layout Design: Hammad [UK]

Cover Art & Page Border Art By: Aalia Tabassum [India]

Internal Artists: Yvette Gilbert [UK] "Ash & Her Cuppa"

Marta Zawrocka [Poland] "Noah's Dream" & "Mahjong Life"

Kissa Maraña [Chile] "Bookstore Gentleman", "Yang Print-Master", "Ali & Ahmed: GQ Lovebirds", "The Gift of Marigold" "Prince William in Motion: 1-6"

My Current Hubby Houston William [USA]: "Jesus Wagon", "JLM Key Chain", "Pug Mug"

Special Thank You To My Ex Hubby, Ricardo Christie [Ireland]: Without his help, listening to the chapters over and over for years on end... this book would never would have been written as it was.

SPECIAL THANK YOU TO MY BEAUTIFUL CHILDREN:

Sienna Sofia

Isabella Maria

Elijah Howard Martin

SPECIAL MENTION TO MY PRECIOUS NIECES & NEPHEWS:

Mila Rey

Grayson Alexander

Michael Todd

Sebastian Wesley

Madelynn Rose

Gideon Stephen

Luke Magnus

Howie Christian

CHILDREN ARE WORTH CHANGING FOR

Let us all commit to change ourselves for the children in our lives...It is with them, for them and through them we see the potential of Heaven for us all.

CONTENTS

FORGIVENESS MEETINGS:

INTRODUCTION

It was a reflective ride. Noah had come a long way since he first found the book, from owning his own car and working for the church to pushing his muscles to their string-bean limits on a motor-less bike and printing things for a living and lots of uncomfortable changes.

Feeling the wind on his face as he peddled idly through the town back to his place was the only thing forcing him to relax despite himself. As he entered the apartment, he could feel the warmth and love; Noah was finally home, and this was his family.

Hank was sitting at the kitchen table looking at his wristwatch as Ash stood facing the kitchen counter, making herself a cup of instant coffee. It was a surreal moment for Noah: The author of the book that changed his life was in his home, drinking his instant, chatting with his houseless friend Hank.

"Hey, Pal! Took you long enough. You are late! You will be happy to know Ash already knows her way around your kitch-en and made us dinner. Hope you like vegan?" Hank spoke as if addressing someone known to him since birth.

Noah wanted this moment to last forever, so, in his true-to-random form, Noah took a mental picture for years to come.

"You alright with aborigine?" Ash stirred a bit of cinnamon and vanilla into Noah's pug mug and then took a seat to the left of Hank.

"Honestly, I have no clue what that even is." Noah had no problem admitting ignorance; he believed it saved everyone time and energy.

"Eggplant," Hank smiled as he took a sip of his Jasmine Tea.

Noah remembered Hank spouting off at the Free Market about drinking coffee with them that evening in celebration, and Noah was not going to let it go for nothing': "Thought you were going to have coffee with us, Hank."

"Yeah...after dinner."

The response was surprising to Noah. Hank was never one to compromise, not even for a woman.

"I've heard about this." Putting his body in motion, taking off Prince William's leash, Noah moseyed over to the kitchen table to join his company, "This is what it must be like if hell freezes over."

The three laughed, and Ash slid her fresh cuppa in front of Noah as a gesture of kindness and affinity for her new kindred spirit.

"So, Noah, I am curious. How did you come to find a copy of my book?" Ash stood up and turned on the hot-water kettle as she pulled out another mug; it was the one Mother bought him when she visited Greece. Noah contemplated her choice of words and coffee receptacle.

"I'm not sure you would approve of who I was when I happened upon your written words." Noah looked down at his coffee, then at the floor.

"Well, I am not sure you would approve of who I was when I wrote the feckin thing." Ash smiled.

Noah thought her Irish accent was entrancing, the "bad words" making her even more so.

Noah shook his head, "doubtful."

"True story," Ash raised her left hand and put her right on top of her coffee cup "Hypocrite to the maximum level." Finishing pouring a new cup, she sat back between her new friends. "I am a firm believer that we preach what we need to learn the most [pause], and then hopefully we learn the lesson before it's too late."

Hank was staying out of this one. Refusing to give his young pal any hint or direction for what he should say or do.

"Fuck it. Fine. If you really want to know..." There was an internal struggle about where Noah felt he should begin. Noah knew where he should start, but he was scared Ash would hate him or at least never look at him the same.

"You tell me yours; I'll tell you mine." Ash winked.

Picking up the perfectly rolled doobie from the centre of the table, Noah lit it up and exhaled to light the embers without just setting fire to the paper. Every movement was a sign of growth and an ever-evolving young man.

"Alright, here goes nothin'. It was a dark and dreary night, and as usual, I was overdressed for the occasion."

Dear Reader,

Before diving into who Noah was and the roads he would take to get to where he ends up (where you find him with Hank and Ash), you need to be made aware of a few things.

First of all: The moments leading up to Noah acquiring the book that would rock his proverbial world were probably some of his ugliest ones. Reaching his personal bottom is not pretty to watch... apologies. However, without understanding his personal deconstruction, you will never fully be in a position to appreciate the beautiful being that is Noah.

Like so many of us today, Noah finds himself lost and drowning in the societal web constructed for us all, which we are told is for our own "good." When he finally stops accepting his daily dose of social medicine and starts to pick up and examine the broken pieces of his socially acceptable life... well, I will let you decide if the change was for the best.

So, without further delay and as your self-appointed story guide, I have decided to soften the blow by recalling such a story from an [mostly] unbiased outsider's point of view. If you must still hate him, love him with that same blind passion. Balance has a way of keeping things in perspective, even if the two sides are sometimes found in the extremes.

Kindest Regards,

Your Devoted Pendulum Writer

Into The Mystic,

Ash

The Church Meeting

"Well, I think it's a good idea. Yes, a thousand is a lot of money for the parish to part with, but we would all benefit. Plus, how exciting to have such a prominent political figure in *our* church!" Sue puffed out her chest as she stood unnecessarily.

Had the world gone absolutely batty?

A thousand bucks for a seminar on how to pay a tax on breathing?

The more Noah thought about it, the worse it got for him in his own mind.

Frustration.

Anger.

Festering at first...

Then rolling into a boil

Are these people all for real?

His face; a placid façade. Not confident he wouldn't explode, Noah excused himself unassumingly.

It was a late-night meeting, and the bathroom down the hallway was next to never used at that hour. The motion-sensor lights turned on after a short flicker. Noah checked under each stall for feet to put his hyper-active mind at ease. He knew no one was there.

Palms - Firmly pressed on the edge of the sink.

Elbows - Locked in tension.

Legs - Dense as marble.

Smooshed father's old Sunday penny loafers, his feet were sweaty and sore after a full day of walking all over the church compound back n' forth. Noah looked right at his reflection, but all he could see was pure hatred. He just got like that sometimes, unable to predict what he'd do or say: removing himself from certain situations [such as this] seemed best. The stupidity of people drove him fucking mad! He hated every single one of them:

Not one of them could last one meeting without looking at their latest electronic devices if they tried, let alone manage to actually give a shit about any one of the many sinners and perceived saints they all gathered to discuss at this Wednesday night meeting; or any of our meetings for that matter! They all just sit there in their fancy suits and dresses. Smug, self-righteous.

Noah took a deep breath and continued his inner monologue with equal passion.

Why would these people even consider inviting a politician and a taxman to speak at our church? LET ALONE PAY THEM TO DO SO!

This tax is a sin all on its own!

Helpful?

Sincere?

Ha! Laughable!

Noah knew he should say something. He also knew it wouldn't make a difference. There was structure when Father was alive and worked at the local worship centre!

There was at least a clear sense of what was right and wrong. That was all gone to the bin and taken straight to the dumpster for disposal.

Compromising beliefs to suit the whims of a sickly society? Where is this world headed? How would Jesus react if He found out His "devoted followers" were in the proverbial bed sheets with the local parasitic tax collectors and corrupt inbred purchased politicians? Jesus was angered when He saw business and politics being conducted in the sacred house of worship of His day.

Noah was expected to not only tolerate it but support it all without question. Satin was present at this Wednesday night meeting, and Noah would take no more part in it. He stared into his own soul...

Seething;

Unable to communicate.

Noah knew full well that each personal agenda they held close to their chests wouldn't allow the ears and the brain to hear his reasonings, even if he channelled the Lord Himself in the dead language of their professed Saviour Jesus Christ.

Nostrils flaring, lips pursed, and jaw clenched.

Then came the out-loud self-talk that was slow and quiet:

"I'm so sick of them! All of them. Our congregation is already hurting, and these idiots want to squeeze the last ounce of blood out of every one of us! For what? A bull shit appearance by our latest political slob. To talk about what? Taxing the poor? Taxing the sick? Taxing us all to breathe fucking air? I'd be surprised if the Bushs, the Koch brothers, or any of the large Monsanto-type corporations actually pay a dime or if we are all expected to cover their pollution too! Since when do these assholes have a monopoly on oxygen? Father warned me about this, and I didn't want to believe it. What a fucking nightmare!"

It was definitely strange, but Noah justified it while comparing his vice to those of others. If the occasional bad word and socially empathetic open eye made him strange, Noah didn't mind.

"The money gathered to help the homeless? What a fucking joke!"

His voice began to raise:

"Not one person, including Mr. G.Q. politician in there, actually gives a shit about the homeless. Common sense dictates that not one single penny of that stupid tax will ever land in the hand of the Homeless Alcoholic Drug-Addicted Schizoid American; as I know, these hypocrites ALL call them outside of the church."

Noah was so angry that it rendered him immobile. He wanted to run, scream and throw something even! But all he could do was stand in that stupid over-teched bathroom. The motion-sensor lights switched off and left the hall in complete darkness. Taking a deep drawn-out breath, Noah ran his fin-

gers and hands over his face and through his hair, trying to shake the hate out of his mind physically.

The lights switched back on.

Unnoticed.

Enough was enough.

He walked back down the long hall, opened the door, and stared at all the self-absorbed **sheeple**. Everyone gradually looked up at Noah.

"You okay there, buddy? You look ill!"

The insurance salesman, Dale, smiled his greasy smile as he did his best to impersonate a sincere human being. Noah wanted to walk over and throw up his left-over Chinese dinner on Dale's slick-rick hair.

"Yeah, I'm not feelin' so good. I'm gonna go home early; sorry, everyone."

Packing up his bag and heading out of the door, he half-heartedly said his farewells:

"Goodnight, everyone. God Bless."

Over the years, Noah got really good at masking his thoughts and feelings.

Business as usual, he thought.

He walked over to his beat-up Jesus-freak wagon, pulled out his "God Loves Me" key chain, and then proceeded with his daily ritual of jimmying his car key in the passenger-side door. He wasn't sure why he even locked it; maybe it was Mother's

voice playing like a broken record in his brain "Safety First, Noah!" It was a piece of crap, but Noah couldn't afford to get any major work done on Mother's hand-me-down station wagon. Heck, he could barely afford his rent these days after the church cut his hours down to three days a week. They told him the church was low on funds and would be using more volunteers to cover his other hours and the hours of most of the full-time staff. Zero-hour contracts were a nightmare of slave-labor proportions, and Noah knew he was being lied to.

1. Add-ons to the church offices cost a pretty penny.

2. He saw the church tithe books only three weeks before.

3. He also knew a few people were giving themselves raises.

But what could Noah do about it? So, as usual, he smiled, said "Thank You," and went home to scream in his pillow. Back to the night of the meeting:

Noah drove through the town on his way back to his apartment. He was still frustrated, and now it was building resentment.

Teeth, fists, and lips were all tightly clenched.

Thoughts of driving into a building crossed his mind. But he quickly reminded himself that his life was God's to take, not his own. Plus, he was too scared to follow through.

Pills?

Not a guarantee that some asshole with a hero complex wouldn't find him and call an ambulance or pump his stomach right there on the spot.

Hanging or wrist slitting?

Too painful and messy also, not a guaranteed sure thing.

Gun?

Not even an option. Knowing Noah's luck, he'd miss, and besides, who would look after his dog and all his potted plants?

By the time Noah had finished talking himself off the ledge, he never would have jumped off; he had realized he was already home. What a horrible day. He honestly wasn't sure if he could take much more of this. He walked his dog to the end of the block and back in a daze. Went inside, loosened the noose he had professionally knotted strategically around his neck, took off his socially acceptable uniform of a suit, and climbed into bed.

Why couldn't life make more sense? With this, Noah finally slept.

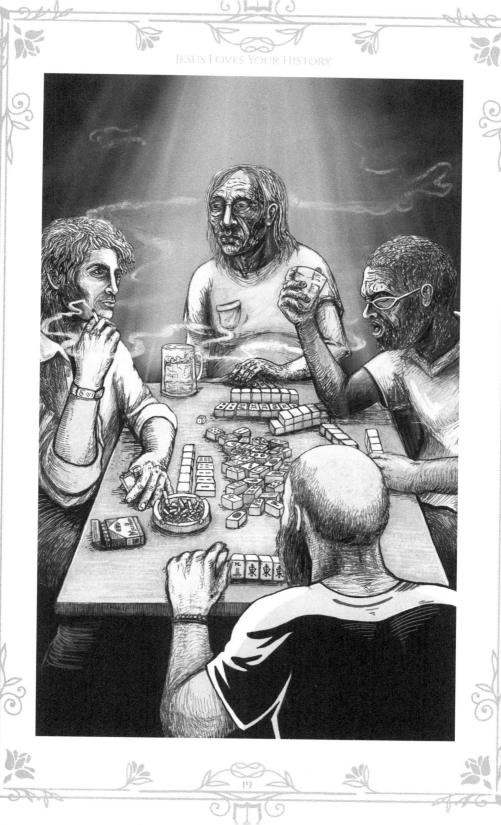

MAHJONG & WHISKEY

On the other side of town, a heated game of Mahjong was underway. Four at the table. Always four. Marble tiles are engraved beautifully with Chinese characters and designs. The men were eight rounds in, and emotions were high as all eight of the men's hands were washing the tiles to prepare for the next round. Moving the tiles face down on the Mahjong table was a ritual, like smoking a cigarette or playing the lotto - a ritual for relief.

It was the backroom of Lucky Palace. It was always the same place, same time, same familiar faces, and same stakes. No Pay? No Play. A gambler's paradise.

It was Tommy's turn to deal, and keeping with tradition, he pressed his hands together, bowing to the table before swiftly breaking down the first wall of tiles.

All was the same as it should be. There was comfort in consistency.

All except one man. One new face.

Usually, a new face at the table didn't upset the balance.

But for whatever reason and the way the stars aligned that particular evening, this new face was off-putting at the very least.

It was more than his face that offset the balance on this particular night.

It was his energy.

Shifty.

Aggressive.

Cocky.

There were certain unspoken agreed-upon codes of conduct.

A sort of "Gentleman's Agreement."

It was unclear whether the young man was unaware of them or just quarrelsome.

Either way, you could cut the tension with a knife that evening; it was that thick.

At first, it was just the young man's energy.

The way he shifted in his seat.

The way he kept saying: "So it's like that!" Anytime a tile was pulled from the centre discard pile.

Smoking was allowed, but the young man was taking it too far.

Light.

Three Puffs.

Stand up, walk behind his chair, lean it, blow his smoke in the centre of the table, sit back down, and put the partly-smoked cigarette out. All just to start this rote behaviour again with a fresh stick of tobacco.

And not just any brand either: Reds; Marlboro Reds!

And when he wasn't smoking, he was playing with his lighter. Flicking the fucking thing and playing with the fire with a maniacal gleam in his eyes.

Tommy was the most zen amongst the three other men at the table. It was as if the young man wasn't even there.

For the other two men at the table, peace wasn't coming so easily to them.

Yee, a middle-aged businessman who was usually the king of calm, started nervously moving his left leg up and down and tapping one of his tiles on the table like an over-caffeinated school boy. Hank, the fourth and most methodical player, appeared to be taking it the hardest. Agitations were brewing.

Hank didn't know how Tommy was able to keep so calm. The young man was pushing Hank's nerves to their callus cold limitations.

Tolerance was almost extinguished.

Playing with fire was the last straw.

Hank was officially triggered.

Desperate to remain calm, Hank flagged down the waiter for another whiskey.

For all the obvious reasons, this was the worst possible choice.

Because, while usually capping himself at four, Hank was well past his magic number, and it was beginning to show. Finishing the short glass as fast as he received it, Hank slammed it on the table. The composed drinker morphed into the damaged alcoholic he normally did his best to hide and would take no prisoners that night.

Shite was about to get real.

A MOTHER'S BOUNDARIES

BANG. BANG. BANG. BANG.

"Noooahhhh, open this door at once! Don't leave your poor Mother outside in this neighbourhood." Noah's Mother had a voice that could curdle milk and probably shatter glass if she put her mind to it. He opened one dry eye and saw a blurry 5:03 a.m. The bright red numbers on his old alarm clock slowly blinked; on, off, on, off... Eye: re-shut.

BANG BANG BANG!

"Noah! If you are not awake, you should be a young man! Early worm! Do I need to call Fred?" Fred was Noah's land-lord, an old friend of Noah's Father. Still lying in bed, an unseen eye-roll took place under his very heavy eyelids. Knowing his options were slim to one, Noah opened his eyes and turned to face his miniature dachshund Prince William who stared back under his little furry eyebrows almost as if to say:

"Is this woman for real?

Doesn't she know what time it is?"

Noah answered back out loud to his pooch:

"I know, buddy, trust me, I know." Out of bed. Shuffle to the door and opened. He usually left his front door unlocked, but he had no interest in arguing with Mother over his safety at five in the morning or any morning for that matter.

"Guten Morgan Mother."

"What's that mean?"

"Maidin Mhaith? Jo Reggelt? Dobre Rano? No? How about Buenos Dias?"

"Speak English, Noah!"

"It means *Good Morning,* Mother. They all mean *Good Morning.*"

Noah could see he was getting nowhere, "Forget it."

Hurling past him, opening all of his blinds, it was as if Noah wasn't even there. One eye still closed, he made his way over to his coffee machine and switched it on;

Obnoxious sounds at war.

Prince William followed Noah into the kitchen, stretched, and yawned as Mother gave her a sharp disapproving look. "What a spoiled dog," she said. "So, what's up, Mother?" Noah replied.

As if ready for her Broadway performance, she spoke her lines with ease: "I went to your father's grave this morning. Do you know what today is? I bet you forgot..."

Noah opened his mouth to answer, but she kept going without breaking for air. "Your *Father* died today, four years ago. Are you going?"

Slight pause.

"You have to visit your father, Noah. When the good Lord takes your dear old Mother, you will not be blessed with these reminders. I swear! If your head wasn't attached to your shoulders, you'd forget that too!"

Theatrical sigh.

"I can't believe you made me swear! Swearing is so very un-christian, Noah! Look what you made your poor Mother do."

Mother was pacing his apartment, looking at every inch with her disapproving eye.

"When was the last time you dusted in here?"

Noah didn't bother trying to answer.

"No matter. I'm heading over to your aunt Judie's. You need to clean this place and go visit your father today. Cleanliness is next to Godliness. You weren't raised in a barn."

Noah's Mother walked quickly over, kissed him on the fore-head, and bee-lined it for the front door, slamming it behind her.

5:20 a.m. and coffee was made.

A relatively painless visit.

Noah couldn't bother himself with getting upset. His Moth-er had no intention of changing. She saw nothing wrong with anything she ever did. She'd done this sort of stuff too many times to count.

Wide awake.

Leash on PW

Grab his coat and cap.

Now was as good a time to walk to town as any. A dough-nut from Smittie's Dough King would make being up this early worth it.

The streets were still dark, almost a ghost town.

Only three lights were on: Street lamp. One store-front that Noah thought was still empty - Smittie's.

The prince, pepped for his morning walk, was smelling everything in sight at nostril level. Noah tugged on the leash and walked them both across the road to check out the well-lit new addition to the town. Peering through the window, he could see an older Gentleman stocking books on a freshly built oak wood bookshelf the length and height of the wall. Front door wide open—Noah decided it looked pretty much open for business and walked them both inside.

The gentleman was standing on a wooden wall ladder whistling and humming "Stairway to Heaven," which blasted through his headphones loud and clear. As if feeling a presence in his shop, the older gentleman spun around, removed his headphones, and smiled wide. Perfect teeth. He was a dashing dresser, very well put together. He looked at Noah and his small dog as if he knew them, the sort of look one gives to long misplaced friends.

"You look lost! Mornin' Son, come on in! I have something for you; a free book for being my first visitor. Come on in! The water's fine, and I ain't no biter." Practically hopping off the ladder, he jogged to the front counter without so much as skipping a beat.

"Dog treats for the little fella?" Noah nodded his head, approving the gesture of kindness.

The gentleman pulled a meat stick from a jar of random treats and tossed it down to Willie—who was standing on his hind legs and happy to partake.

PW had a new best friend.

"How's life, Sir?"

Initially shocked at being referred to as a "Sir," Noah took a moment to reflect before laying his woe on his new cosmic friend's shoulders.

"Complicated."

Noah then looked him square in the eye:

"A bit depressing, actually. You?"

With a twinkle of knowing, the gentleman replied heartily,

"Amazing! Absolutely fantastic, after subtracting all the things no one seems to care about anyway, like the fact that if an asteroid a decent enough size hits our beautiful life ball, we're all burnt toast anyway." A curious chuckle arose from his diaphragm as he dove into Noah's soul with a carefree glance.

The Gentleman continued, as Gentleman do:

"Alright, I think I have just the book for you. I sense you're a fellow idealist, so you'll like this author. I'm sure of it."

First checking the shelf near the register, then shuffling through the medium-sized box on the floor next to the counter....

"Ah, here we are!"

The older Gentleman handed a book to Noah. It looked like the cover was made from recycled paper bags, and all it said on it in all lower-case letters was: "A book by: me."

After handing Noah the book, the Gentleman smiled as he walked back to his ladder, leaving poor confused Noah with his thoughts.

"Don't worry, Sir. It will all make more sense in the end."

As the older Gentleman was just about to put his headphones back on, he stopped and glanced over his shoulder so as to be heard clearly:

"Life is shit, and then you die, there is, or there isn't meaning to your living; all I know is this, till my last dying breath, I will continue to plant apple trees if only for the fuck of it my dear Sir. Every problem can be solved. It is just a matter of being brave enough to try and selfless enough not to worry about what's in it for you at that moment. Read the book. The author is brilliant and beautifully optimistic for such a pessimist. And as for asteroids annihilating life as we know it, it doesn't have to be that way. There is always a solution when powerfully intelligent minds set their ego aside for the greater good. But Son, we have to give these great minds a reason to fight for us, and you, reading that right there, what you have in your hand, I believe is one step closer to saving all our souls. It just takes one. And Sir, never doubt that one isn't you. Enjoy and don't come back till you finish what you came here for. And be ready to report, or I will never sell you one of my books as long as we both shall live. Have a great morning!"

Headphones promptly back on, the conversation was clearly over whether Noah wanted it to be or not. Noah turned around absolutely baffled and more confused than when he entered that oak fortress of knowledge and wisdom. Asteroids? A book to change the world?

Led Zeppelin Karaoke? None of it made any sense.

Noah slowly turned, walked out of the town's new book-store, and headed back home. Overwhelmed with a sense of peace for what seemed like the first time, Noah was determined to understand what that older Gentleman was talking about. Smittie's; a distant memory. A new gift in hand.

"Strange morning," he said to his short-legged friend.

The winds shifted in his soul. A new dawning was on the horizon.

Change was a-comin'.

Ready or Not.

BREATHE...

He was five years old again. Both parents were towering over him in church. They were telling him he would lead the future generations closer to heaven on earth.

His little heart started pounding with fear.

"I cannot lead!"

"I am far from being good enough!"

"I cannot even control my own feelings half the time."

"Can't you hear me?"

"I'm only five!"

[Noah was quite a self-aware young man in this dream]

"How can I lead anyone anywhere if I don't know where I'm going?"

"This is insane!"

Fear building inside.

His parents moved in closer, gliding toward their frightened child, pushing an entire future on him without even consulting him first! He wasn't even close to being able to do what they asked of him. Didn't they care? Why were they not listening or understanding?

Would they have bothered to listen to him if he was any other age? Would his future age earn him the respect he could not get while still five? Age should NOT matter!

Noah found himself running, constantly looking over his shoulder.

His parents were gliding faster!

He ran straight off a cliff...

Falling...

Stomach dropping...

His tiny heart quieted...

Moment of Peace.

"This must be what birds feel like."

Falling to his death. The fear morphed into a level of acceptance.

As his poor little child-sized heart stopped, he awoke.

"Give A Dog A Bone" HWF

THE FIRST STEP

Mouth wide open, screams replaced by gasps for fresh air. It was a beautiful crisp morning, birds chirping poetically out his window. Grasping for moments, trying to remember his dream and trying to make sense of it. Looking around, Noah stopped. Gazing at his own tired reflection through the half-opened bathroom door in the mirror above his rusted sink.

Geeze, I look beaten.

He looked old, even to himself. Misery was written all over his face.

Do I honestly think no one else can see this?

Sitting up in bed, he fixed his pillow and stretched to reach "a book" that the kind older Gentleman gave him just two mornings ago.

His third morning - already halfway through. Noah was engrossed in every beautifully ideal thought the author expressed. His own notes were written in the margins, and questions were written on different coloured post-its, some marked "Pages of Significance." It was 8 a.m., and after that crazy dream, he needed guidance. *Ritualistic Bibliomancy;* some people at his church called it "Bible-dipping," but this wasn't that Bible. Have a question? Close your eyes, point, open your eyes, read = Solution! After a dream like that, Noah was willing to try anything. Closing his eyes, focusing on his desire for some sense of direction, praying for insight: He placed "a book" flat on his left hand, right hand gently resting on the cover. Randomly opening "a book" pointing to a page. He slowly opened his eyes to read:

"Meditation Park"

Looking at his hound dog even more confused, he thought out loud:

"How's this meant to be helpful?"

Just to be sure, he started reading the section. As expected, nothing stood out as useful—a pointless exercise. *Sure,* (Noah internally argued with himself) *a local Meditation Park would be nice and relaxing on a morning such as this, but I need a MIRACLE, not another dream.*

Noah needed the sort of miracle brought about by making a real life-changing decision. But what could he change? Tense anxiety. He swiped the book off his lap onto the floor with a heavy, deep sigh, startling his dog into a riled-up bark monster. Ears flying in the air like a super-hero-hound, Prince William jumped off the bed, landed, and tripped over the book, knocking it open. Noah flung half his body over the side of his bed, hoping his dog wasn't hurt. PW was fine; sitting next to the book, looking up at his frazzled owner, then looking at the open pages:

"The First Personal Step: Forgiveness Meetings"

A smile crept over Noah's lips.

"You are an instrument of the Lord, Willie, Good Dog!"

Twenty minutes after receiving his divine "instruction," Noah shuffled to his kitchen and poured a steaming cup of his favourite organic blend into his pug of a mug. The pug's face was overly happy, wide-eyed, and ready for the day; Noah wasn't there yet. Nostrils resting over the ledge of his coffee cup, he took several deep meditative breaths; waking up slowly was a nice indulgence. Twenty-four years old, looking like an eighty-year-old. Noah had the world resting firmly on his shoulders, whether he liked it or not, and this was *not* gravity's fault. As he was glancing over at his calendar, there were two very distinct choices for his day:

One: *Stick with his weekly Saturday church appointments*

[Easy, comfortable, and familiar yet killing his soul at a pretty steady pace]

Two: *Try out the First Personal Step in "a book."*

[WAY out of his comfort zone, unfamiliar, and downright scary... but he wasn't sure it could be much worse than his first option]

He took a long drag from his vaporizing pen, and then, surprising even himself, he chose what was behind door number two. After having portions of that same creepy nightmare three nights in a row, Noah knew something had to change, and it had to change today! Taking his first sip of coffee goodness, it dawned on him that this was perhaps the rarest of occasions when the church was not only NOT going to help, it was making the perceived problems larger than need be. He was beginning to equate church with judgment and hypocrisy, and Noah wanted no part in either. He couldn't change them his way, and they couldn't help him with theirs.

The decision was made.

The first of many that day.

EPIPHANY

Spending quite a while checking pockets and cushions for any chance he could scrounge up; Noah took a step back and asked God for guidance. He needed to step away from the situation. The shower was on, and scalding hot water began running through the rickety pipes. Pain and pleasure were balanced. Hands pressed up against the tiled wall. Water pouring down his forehead, nose, lips, and chin... mind blank.

"Tithe!"

The guidance he was looking for. He felt strong and justified; he was on a holy mission!

Hot turned to cold. Shower off. Towel dry. Putting on his Sunday best, he then took to raiding his weekly tithe jar. Noah was now ready to go, counting it down to the cent and dumping every penny into his coat pocket. Keys, leash, bag... the pair headed out the front door; heads held high in excitement.

Purpose!

PRINTING SHOP PROPORTIONS

The local printers were the first stop on Noah and the Prince of Pup's list of places to be that day.

Happy resolve oozed from every pore. The door chimed for the store's first visitors of the day.

"Hello, Yang. I need a few copies of something."

The town's Master printer accepted the book from Noah's hands, glancing nonchalantly at the pages marked. Still silent. Noah spoke again,

"I can only afford three dollars' worth."

"Noah, why not put it on the church account?" Noah fell quiet. Yang pushed further, "I just put on that for you."

Happy resolve soon turned into an uncomfortable nervousness.

"Actually, this is a personal project, Yang. I have to pay cash. I just CAN NOT afford more than three bucks on this. I need the rest to buy some chairs."

Squinting his eye in professed disbelief, Yang was not convinced.

"Still, sounds like a church project. Church account okay."

Yang was insisting at this point, and Noah could see confusion in his deep, dark, enlivened eyes. Noah could not and would not justify using the church account, so he put the three dollars in cash on the counter in front of Yang, looking him dead straight in the eyes for the first time in twenty-four years.

"I'll be back in an hour or so. See how many you can make for me, and DON'T USE THE CHURCH'S ACCOUNT! PLEASE! God Bless Yang. Thank you."

An hour came and went like nothing. Garage Sale after Yard Sale, Noah managed to find what he was after: Thirteen random beach chairs and his ten dollars were gone. Barely able to fit in the Christ-mobile, Noah and the hound headed back to Yang's. It was 10 o'clock and his day felt half gone, time was flying by, and his first Forgiveness Meeting had not even started yet.

Yang was outside having a cigarette with his Smittie's doughnut holes and black coffee; one brown sugar cube

It seemed like everyone had a ritual just to breathe easier these days.

Without a word, Yang handed Noah the bag; two dozen holes and one strawberry sprinkle doughnut were left untouched. Noah knew which one was for him. Yang knew Noah, perhaps even better than Noah knew himself: Strawberry with sprinkles had been his favourite since he was a small boy. And Smitties made the best, hands down—Crispy on the outside with a soft, warm centre.

Still silent, Yang handed Noah a fresh coffee. Knowing it took about eight minutes to walk to Smittie's from Yang's, Noah figured Yang was either done with the pamphlets or never started

them at all. Suppressing anxiety, embracing the kind gesture, Noah pulled out his vape pen and took a couple of drags to show he was relaxed and confident, even though he was far from either of those feelings one could get.

Watching Yang's lips, fingers, eyes, and chest all move with the rhythm of Noah's long-lost favourite habit. He caught himself and physically shook the thought from his mind. Yang was no blind man.

"You want?" Yang gestured toward his bag of tobacco.

"Nope, I've got a year under my belt," Noah replied

"You still smoking, Noah," Yang laughed.

"Yeah, one-thousandth of the chemicals! Vaping's healthier, Yang."

Noah bit into his strawberry sprinkle heaven; his mouth was as full as it could get, "I've been breathing better since I swapped."

Swig of coffee to knock back the half-chewed bite, "I don't wake up hacking and coughing anymore. Wanna try it out?"

Yang smirked and shook his head as if to say, "no, thanks."

Cigarette crackled with a deep pull from his lips. "Okay," he spoke on the exhale. The ashtray was put to good use. Two holes pushed into his hole, careful not to lose a flake of sugary goodness. He then gestured for Noah to go ahead inside as he pulled a dog treat from his pocket. Dropping his body down like a frog onto the balls of his feet while dusting a bit of sugar on his pants from his one free hand, Yang strategically placed the treat in the centre of that palm extending his arm just enough to entice the prince. Willie took the jerky beef square

slowly and gently with his sharp yet selective canines. With a pat on the head, Yang immediately sprang back up, grabbed his human treats of coffee and doughnut holes, spun around, and followed Noah back inside his shop.

Pamphlets were already done; Noah could see them lying on the counter in a perfect stack. Yang handed Noah his copy of "a book" back.

"I make thirteen tri-fold. You don't mind; I took the first quote and put it in front, so it looks nice. I use more expensive paper. You are a good customer with church always. I make nothing on this one."

Walking around to the other side where his cash register had sat for years, Yang pulled out his own copy of "a book."

"Noah, you have big balls. I no expect. Need more, I make. No problem, book, brother." A wink and a nod to finish his thought.

Dread crept into Noah's already over-active anxiety-ridden mind. He couldn't hide any of this from Yang. Went there with Mother every Friday to make copies of colouring sheets for children's mass; Yang had known Noah since he was a small boy.

What was worse?

Yang knew Mother too well.

"Uhh, Yang? Can you keep this our little secret? Mother would not approve of my quoting any book that wasn't the good one, and I honestly don't think the folks at church would understand either. I'm not ready to hear how disappointed God would be with me... you know Mother better than most; she wouldn't get it."

"Yah, yah, yah. Lips sealed. She'd flip!" Yang replied.

Opening his copy of "a book," Yang cleared his throat to quote the quoted Dalai Lama:

"According to Buddhism, reflecting on the reality of suffering never induces either pessimism or despair. It leads to the discovery of the root causes of our plight: Desire, hatred, and ignorance, and to a way of freeing ourselves from them. By 'ignorance,' we mean not understanding the true nature of people and things. It gives rise to the other two poisons. When ignorance dissolves, desire and hatred have no foundation, and the source of our suffering has dried up; as a result, we experience spontaneously altruistic happiness that is no longer at the mercy of negative emotions."

Closing the book and gently placing it back under his register, Yang smiled knowingly.

It was like he understood that "something" Noah was searching for so desperately; he understood Noah's fear of what those currently closest to him would think. Not only because he knew those people but because Yang had experienced something similar at one point in his own life not so very long ago.

Noah was clearly scared.

"Do you want to be happy, Noah?" Yang said.

He nodded his pitiful head, "yes."

"Allow it. You are a good man; now go. I miss my show."

Yang gave his diplomatic goodbye nod and a smile you could feel even if he didn't let it show in the form of raised lips and pearly-white chompers.

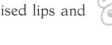

Noah set off for the park.

Scared to death.

But resolute.

FACING THE FEAR

Just for the record:

Noah had marched in front of abortion clinics, preached the word of the Lord on street corners, handed out pocket-sized Bibles to the homeless, and prayed with the young women and men of the night as they walked their tracks. He'd done all this and much more since he was a small boy, a current veteran witness at age twenty-four. But all that seemed easy now compared to what he was gearing up to do by himself in the park that afternoon.

Starting his very first Forgiveness Meeting all by his lonesome. Noah knew people were going to think he was a lunatic. But there was no turning back at this point. Noah's mind started to race. What if someone I know sees me?

He couldn't think about that now; it was too late. The park's parking area was absolutely packed on a warm, beautiful Saturday afternoon! Noah was about to exit the lot in search of street parking—then as if by fate, a young couple pulled out of the best spot in the whole place.

Another divine sign?

Perfect parking job. Engine off, and the prince crawled out from under the driver's seat, hopping up on Noah's lap and jumping excitedly into his face, licking his nose, waiting impatiently for his adventure. Doors open. Noah began to drag out all the random beach chairs from his beat-up "Jesus wagon," leaning them haphazardly against the front hood on the sidewalk. Looking around, he noticed all eyes were on him. Actually, they were all glued to the Bible verses that enveloped his station wagon. From the well-known "Jesus Loves You" all the way to the powerful verses from Revelations discussing the end of times.

Noah had never felt this before:

Embarrassment.

Wishing he found street-side parking, he quickly grabbed as much as he could carry and started off toward the pond near the centre of the park. Prince William pulled with all his strength in any direction his little legs could muster, beach chairs clanging and smashing into his knees and thighs. It was the longest few meters of Noah's life, and he definitely wasn't turning back now.

A MEETING FOR ONE

Destination reached. The random beach chairs were unfolded in a circle around the ancient-looking willow tree next to the pond positioned in the centre of the park. Noah found a few pebbles the size of abnormally large lighters that he found useful in pinning the Forgiveness Meeting Pamphlets to each seat.

He couldn't stop thinking about the coincidence:

I had thirteen dollars.

I used ten of them and got thirteen random beach chairs.

And the rest was given to Yang to make pamphlets.

Which he made thirteen of.

Noah had no idea he would get thirteen chairs or that Yang would make exactly thirteen pamphlets. And he most certainly did not know exactly thirteen large pebbles would be right where he needed them on the windiest day of the spring season. Thirteen... Why thirteen? Yet he was no believer in coincidence; his vocabulary had no such thing. He was filled with a sense of Hope. A calm peace rushed through him instantaneously.

Lord.

Give me strength.

Be my personal armor against sin and impure thoughts.

He felt good. Really good. He knew he was doing the right thing. Attempting to actually do the first step in "a book" by at-

tending Forgiveness Meetings required a physical commitment. It also required the ability to face one's fears head-on.

This was scary, and again Noah was rendered immobile for several minutes. Opening "a book" and curling up with his mighty little dog under the willow tree, all he could bring himself to do was read and reread the first section.

That was it. A strong feeling of flight duking it out with his urge to fight through his fear took place internally.

Then, almost instantly, something clicked in his brain, and he understood!

This book is about action, about change. It is not just for observation like most other books shelved all over the world!

Indeed, this thought, this singular thought, appeared to be paralyzing him. Noah was told repeatedly that life was what it was, and he needed to live it the way he was told to, or he would shame his family and end up in a place called hell. Shame? Hell? Deep down, none of this made any sense at all to Noah. The world he grew up in wasn't even close to being perfect, heck! Half the time, it wasn't even tolerable!

So, there he was, back against that old willow tree's trunk, daydreaming about how the world could be if everyone made little adjustments. Little adjustments he knew firsthand were excruciatingly hard to make. Time began to pass quite slowly.

Noah stood up, dusted himself off, and decided to start. Choosing the faded blue beach chair closest to the pond. It had one of its flat rubber bars that were supposed to give "seat support" missing. Noah had to readjust his rear end repeatedly to

avoid slipping through onto the soggy wet grass. Noah thought through the whole scenario:

If someone falls through this chair,
I'd never hear the end of it and not one person
Would stay for another meeting again.

So, Noah took that chair and suffered the consequences. He sat at that meeting for a while. By himself on a broken, faded beach chair. In a circle with twelve other beach chairs around a tree. An excited dog tied to the willow tree, barking loudly at the birds up above, getting up to fix the circle here and there when the wind ripped through, knocking down a few of the chairs once in a while. Noah thought to himself: I forgive my-self for not attending church today. And then he thought:

Now's as good a time to start the meeting as any.
I am deciding to start with myself.
I have some forgiveness
I need to give and receive...
I don't need other people to start the dialogue in my mind.
As long as I'm not talking out loud to myself, no one will
Think I'm crazy, Hopefully ;)

Whether or not that was sound logic, it was good enough for Noah.

He began by coming up with a list of the top five things he wanted to address at this first Forgiveness Meeting:

One: I would like to forgive myself for worrying so much
about what other people think of me.
Two: Maybe forgive myself for living my life for other people,
mainly Mother.
Noah took a deep breath and continued his meeting within his

own head:

Three: Forgive my parents; they know not what they've done.

Four: I will forgive myself for being so blinded by my ignorance and fears.

And...

Five: Forgive myself... forgive myself for not having it all figured out by now.

This horrible feeling came over him. He was a failure.

HANK THE HOUSELESS MAN

He spent his life "Colouring within the lines," doing what he was told was correct even when certain "right" things didn't sit well with him. Justifying his anger and hatred toward others who lived in what he was told was "sin," ignoring any pain or unfortunate circumstance that may have led these "sinners" astray.

A blanket of generalized hatred.

Sitting alone, facing his trusting dog still barking up the willow tree, constantly thinking about his rear-end slipping through the hole he was sitting on, surrounded by empty beach chairs, Noah started to really question his existence:

Why the fuck am I here?

His thoughts honed in on the illogic of it all:
If I say the word "fuck," I'm going to hell and living in sin!
Is that even realistic?
I know "fuck" is an aggressive-sounding word but hell?
Honestly?

It seemed to Noah like the more he learned about what was expected of him by his religion and culture and the more he saw what was going on in the world around him, the more confused he became about it all. The expectations and realities seemed so far off from each other that none of it was making any sense!

His thought continued:
Since hindsight is 20/20... then right now, looking back, I

think it would make more sense if people who took from the poor and gave to the rich were reminded of fire and brimstone compared to those who were saying the 'F' word. I just don't see how a word is more "hell-bound" than kicking people while they are down.

Noah Paused.

Then again, when I stood out in front of the abortion clinics holding signs about these women being killers... saying I was kicking these ladies while they were down is an understatement. I mean, at least when the rich were raping and pillaging the poor, they didn't hold signs up calling them killers, bound for the fires of hell. Or maybe raping and pillaging is enough damage done and doesn't require a sign.

He was headed down a very negative train of thought. Noah had to be very careful because this was exactly why he was here in the first place.

*I don't want to be like this
Something has to change!*

He looked around.
It was about 3 o'clock in the afternoon. Noah had sat, by himself, for a few hours at that point, beginning to feel a bit discouraged.

*Should I pack this all up and try again tomorrow?
Should I have made a sign?
The only people around here are homeless alcoholics.
I should have picked a better park.*

He decided to give it another few minutes. Pulling out his watch, staring at it as the second hand went around in circles,

before he knew it, the clock struck half-past-three, and that was it. Noah stood up and started gathering the pamphlets. The pebbles used to hold down the pamphlets on each beach chair were placed in a circle around the willow tree trunk; he figured he could use them again in the morning if he couldn't find a better spot to hold the next meeting at.

"Hey, you. Buddy?"
Noah heard the man but didn't reply.

"Hey, Pal." The man persisted, "what time you got there?"

For an instant, excitement! Was this what Noah was waiting for? He turned around with a smile, ready to start his rehearsed explanation on Forgiveness Meetings. Noah's heart sank; a tinge of fear set it. It was one of those homeless people reeking of whiskey. Which made Noah think:

A bit pricey for someone without a home.

Then he reasoned with himself that if one did not have a home, it would, in turn, leave them with more cash to buy a good bottle of Jameson. Noah started to get a bit angry and strangely jealous about that, trying his best to shake off the judgmental thoughts, but they just kept pouring into his cerebral cortex. Looking at the old wind-up watch on his bony wrist, it read 3:33 p.m., exactly 3:33 p.m. To the minute, most likely even the second at the rate Noah's day was going. Coincidence? Who knew? All he could think about was the man's myriad smells, simply asking for the time.

Who are you to judge this man, Noah?
Get out of your head!

"It's 3:33 p.m. exactly," Noah said with a fake smile.

"You don't say? I would guess it was later by the looks of that sky, but clearly, I've been wrong before!"

The dishevelled man laughed at his own joke; you could tell he was used to it. Noah wasn't sure if it was rude to laugh or not laugh so he half smiled and awkwardly passed the man a pamphlet. The homeless man didn't ask for a pamphlet, but Noah didn't know how to respond, so by giving it to the man, he hoped it would change the subject or, at best, scare the man away for the moment till Noah could gather his things and skedaddle. No dice.

"What's this? Some religious nuts-o-futz-o stuff?" The man scrunched up his face as though offered chicken feet for the first time.

That wasn't a reaction Noah was prepared for, but it was honest, that was for sure.

"Not really. It actually has nothing to do with religion, can you read?"

"Just because I smell of Jack and piss doesn't make me illiterate, pal."

"Sorry if I offended you. I tend to be a bit insensitive; I was trying this social experiment I have been reading about in this book. The first step is all about participating in a Forgiveness Meeting, so I figured I would start one myself. I was expecting more people to show up."

"How many people came?" The man said.

"Well, just me so far and now you," Noah replied.

Walking over to the chairs on the far side of the willow tree, Noah started folding them up one by one. He wasn't in a hurry, so when the man sat on his broken, faded beach chair and picked up the book. Noah decided to take his time and give him a chance to rest. Plus, he was half curious if the man realized it was broken and if the man's butt would fall straight through it. Leaving two chairs and his dog tied to the tree, Noah decided to take a risk and start walking a few of the beach chairs back to his Jesus wagon. If the guy took the book or his dog, the lesson would be learned for next time. Noah had a funny feeling that this particular smelly homeless man was not what he seemed. Like he had met a spiritual guide or prophet and was being tested somehow.

It took a while to walk back to the car with four chairs clanging against each of his knees hanging from his forearms. By the time Noah walked back, he could see from a distance that the dog leash was no longer around the tree!

How could I have been so stupid?
What would possess me to trust a man who
Doesn't even have a stable place to live!!!

Walking faster, then practically runny, Noah was blinded by fear, anger, and sadness.

Then he stopped.

He knew he was wrong. Wrong to the point of embarrassment. As he looked on the other side of the tree, there was PW; he was jumping on the homeless guy's face and licking his nose. The two of them looked like they had been friends for a lifetime. PW hated most people. Of all the people to decide to finally like, he chose the smelliest, dirtiest man in

the city! There was a lesson in all this. There had to be. But all Noah could think about was the smell of piss and whiskey rubbing off on his small dog's coat. Going back and forth between guilt for having such judgmental thoughts and wishing the guy would just leave already, so he didn't have to feel so uncomfortable: Noah justified all this with the fact that he didn't even have a dollar to give the man if he wanted to. None of it made any sense; even he knew that on some basic level. Deep down, he knew there was more to this man than how he smelled and looked. Noah could see the fading twinkle of wisdom that wasn't quite beaten out of him yet. Always prepared: Noah had an extra Bible in the wagon and an extra travel blanket. Guilt eating away at his insides, Noah wanted to give this man something so that he didn't feel like a jerk when he left the man alone to face the night. Was that self-righteous? What would Jesus have done? He couldn't very well just invite some strange, smelly homeless guy into his home just because he was nice to his dog. Noah was feeling a little guilty about having his initial judgy-mac-judgerson episode.

So, Noah did what he usually did whenever he got awkward or uncomfortable; he started to preach:

"When was the last time you went to the house of God in search of forgiveness for your sins?"

"I thought you said this wasn't religious? Was that just a trick? I thought this whole circle thing was for forgiveness, and now you are telling me I got to go to church and all that shit? Look, Pal, going to church is all fine and dandy when you have something to give those folks but when you look like me? Well, let's just say I have seen more back doors of

churches than front doors. So, what's really going on here?" The man continued to pet the prince, not moving an inch.

"I apologize." A few minutes of reflective silence. Then Noah continued, "I'm just going to be brutally honest. You make me uncomfortable. I am not used to being around homeless people unless I am dishing out food at the pantry behind the church. What I am doing here isn't religious. But I am. I am doing this Forgiveness Meeting thing because I feel lost, unhappy and stuck. Have you ever felt that way? I mean, I even had a meeting at church, and I didn't even show up today. I came here instead."

Noah took a seat against the willow's trunk, completely deflated.

"Something has to change in my life, Sir, or I will keep drowning in my guilt and regrets. I literally have gotten to the point where I pretty much hate everyone, and any time someone lies or cheats or steals, I have this intense urge to shake them and scream at them for bringing our world down to the pits of hell with their actions. There is something severely wrong with that. And the kicker is, most of my family and a good portion of the congregation I belong to are pretty much all the same way. I'm beginning to feel sick about the whole thing. I'm not even sure why I am alive anymore. What's the point?"

Noah couldn't believe he said all that! It was as if he was just finishing clawing at his own skin and scrapping it all off so this stranger could see the ugliness of his insides. Noah got even more uncomfortable. Standing up, he went over to grab the book and the pamphlets from the man's hands. "Forget it; it's stupid. Just forget all of it."

The man blocked him without any sign of aggression. "Whoa, whoa, whoa there, buddy. Stop right there, take a seat." The man motioned for Noah to sit next to him. Hesitating, Noah sat on the edge of the red flower-print beach chair, trying not to be his usual rude self.

"Look, Pal, not one of us is perfect. We should all be slowing down and humbling ourselves because we are not the only ones on this big ball of rocks. As far as I can tell, we are all just a bunch of selfish assholes running around screaming, 'look at me! Give me what I want, and look at me!' I'm not trying to be funny or anything, but look at me! [chuckling] I am a mess of a human being. You would never think for one second that I used to have more than one house, a beautiful wife, and a great career. We are all roaming this planet in search of reason, purpose, or a personality ha-ha. Personally, I could use a bit of forgiveness myself. I haven't even been able to look at myself in a mirror, any mirror, for years now. I have nightmares about meeting anyone from my past life, laughing at the pathetic old man I have become, tellin' me how great life got once I left. Now, if I can't even look at myself in a godforsaken mirror, what makes you think I would step foot in a building where judgment and fear fester?"

Getting defensive, Noah blurted out:
"We're not all that bad! We help people!"

With an eyebrow raised, the man took a deep breath, mustering up as much empathy as he could; he went on:

"Really? By the looks of it, you couldn't wait to get rid of me. What kind of 'help' is that? I could see it in your face; you thought I took off with your dog just a few minutes ago. You automatically assumed that since I smelled of whiskey and piss,

I could and would steal from you. Like it's a reflex for people in my circumstances."

"I never said that," Noah replied.

"You're telling me that if I sat next to you in your beloved church, you wouldn't slide down to the other end of the bench or crinkle your nose and make a comment to anyone who would listen? Doubtful Pal."

Defensively shrivelling under the truth, Noah stood up and took a seat next to his smelly new friend. The truth began to flow from his twenty-four-year-old lips: "You are probably right. Your smell is driving me up the wall, and I have wanted you to leave since the moment you arrived. I am sorry for being so rude and transparent."

"Was that so hard to admit? Pal, look, I forgave you the moment I saw your expression. I'd also hate my smell if I wasn't used to it. In fact, I partially smell like this on purpose. It keeps folks from getting too close, like a sorta safety bubble. Works pretty good, doesn't it?"

A light chuckle broke the mood, and they both relaxed.

"If you don't mind me being honest and working through my judgments, I don't mind if you decide to join in on this Forgiveness Meeting with me tomorrow. I promise no force-fed religion. By the way, what's your name Sir?"

"There is that 'Sir' again, huh? Well, uh, you can call me Hank."

"My name is Noah, and I would be honoured if you would show up. I will be here from eleven to three."

The man named Hank thought about it. "I guess I could clear my schedule."

As Noah would very soon learn:

Hank was a stickler about his schedule
And boy did he have one.

AN EVENING SERVICE

After Noah's first Forgiveness Meeting, he took his time getting back to the empty apartment called home. Mentally rehearsing his best "sick" cough for that evening's service was just part of a plan to miss tomorrow's Sunday morning mass and Mother's direct and imposing disapproval. Noah considered both of these pseudo sacrifices well worth making, considering present circumstances.

In order to survive the week, he knew a cameo appearance at tonight's service with a "sick" cough was a must, hence the "sick" cough practice. Noah figured if he could fool the folks tonight, word would get back to Mother, and she might leave him be for a day or two. Noah found himself daydreaming as he was getting changed; *what would it be like if he stayed home to nap and bark at cats through the window while Prince William suffered through that evening's service?* But then compassion set in. Not wishing his ridiculously pointless existence on anyone, let alone the only living being he cherished.

Noah decided he'd suffer through it for both their sakes. After putting on Father's old penny loafers as if for the last time, Noah turned to his hound dog:

"I'll be back shortly, William. Enjoy your nap for both of us. Hey Will? You wanna go to church for me, and I'll nap for you?" He said, half-jokingly.

PW crawled further under the blanket on the couch and gruffed in reply.

"I guess that's a no."

Laughing as he grabbed his jacket and started down his front steps to his still running Jesus Wagon, Noah could hold it in no longer; he began laughing hysterically to the point of tears: One of the very few benefits of having a vehicle no one wanted and in the POS category, was that even if it was left running, on a Saturday night, in the centre of one of the roughest neighbourhoods, no one—AND I REPEAT NO ONE—wanted to be caught dead taking his ride for a ride! Fashionably late, Noah hit the road, still crying from laughter.

"Noah, you're late, man. Where were you today? You missed the outreach meeting. Don't worry; I took notes for yah! We put you in charge of the booth next Saturday with Yolanda. We figured you wouldn't mind I..." Randy was interrupted.

"SHHHhhhhhh" An uptight newly born again made it very clear he was there for worship.

"I saved you a cupcake. That politician brought them in."

Randy unwrapped his booty of cupcake treasures showing Noah what he believed he missed out on.

"SHHHHHHHHHHHHUUUUUUUUUUsssshhhhhhhhhh!"

The juiced-up Jesus look-a-like put his gigantic hand on Randy's shoulder and unleashed his best pre-religious death stare on the two men talking in front of him, giving the impression that they better follow suit and shut their mouths or face the wrath of more *shushing*. Noah looked down at the huge Satan tattoo that took over the man's entire forearm. He could see that Jesus holding a sword to the Devil's throat was a new addition based on the clarity of the ink and bright colours of the sword compared to the dull Satanic horns and pointed tongue. Not wanting to upset the grizzly bear any further, Noah apologized and signalled to Randy to cut it out.

Randy was in Noah's outreach group. They met every Saturday afternoon to plan their weekly event in any town [that hadn't banned them yet] within a hundred-mile radius. Noah missed today's meeting to start his first Forgiveness Meeting. Randy had no idea, and Noah planned on keeping it that way. Randy was about twenty-eight years old, four years older than Noah, but the pecking order wasn't based on age. Leadership in the outreach group was determined by how on "fire" one was for the Lord's word. You could say Noah was on "fire" with regards to the word of the Lord, active in practicing what he was taught to preach. Up till that point, Noah had not been beaten. Noah attended every meeting, knew every Bible verse, and not only participated in every church outreach but started most of them.

By the time the night service was over, Noah had mentally gone through every scenario he could think of for the following Saturday's event. The two most likely outcomes ended with him feeling like a total hypocrite. He thought to himself:

Option one;

So, I show up, help them set up for an event I don't agree with in the first place, stand at a booth, and promote our outreach group with Yolanda—a woman who would probably rob a blind homeless man while preaching the Good Word of our Lord and Saviour, then justify that stealing the man's money was doing him some sort of a favour somehow—

Then I'd probably be asked to do the entire event clean-up so the rest of the Wednesday night group could go out to dinner with that grease-ball politician and slithering tax collector guy to chat more about how they can work the system so they can avoid paying the full carbon tax they spent the whole day selling to the rest of the congregation as a "great idea" and "the work of the Lord."

Bull shit.

Option two;

I show up a bit later, so I don't get stuck doing all the setup work while the fat, lazy, self-righteous slobs schmooze with our pastor and the "guests of honour" still get stuck in the outreach booth with Yolanda, the know-it-all Queen of the liars still get stuck on clean up, and still leave pissed off.

Option three;

I somehow grow a pair of balls and tell them that taxing the already over-taxed for breathing is wrong and that politics and religion have no business mixing.

Or maybe I get really lucky, and a semi-truck drives two hundred miles an hour straight into my broken-down scrap-metal of a wagon, killing me instantly and putting me out of my misery before the event even starts.

Noah knew that the third scenario was just as likely as the fourth; his backbone was made of silly puddy. So, after mass, when Randy went over the details of the following Saturday's sacrilegious event at a safe enough distance from the ex-hell's angels dude, Noah put on his best fake smile and told his friend

he'd, of course, be there. Randy gave him a big hug with a wholesome:

"God Bless" and a "See you next Saturday, brother!"

Then walked over to the hot new converts that had just joined the "Human Trafficking Awareness" group; there was no doubt that he was going to try to bring them over to the "Church Outreach," that was Randy; always randy. Anyway, back to Noah: Exhaling and loosening his tie; thinking the worst of it was over, and then---

"Hey NOAH!!!!"

Shit.

I can't stand you, woman!

You ruin everything good.

I don't think I will make it through a full day in that booth with just you.

Noah knew that if he said half of the things, he thought to himself, well, let's just say his face would be red from slaps.

"Hello, Yolanda. How is Jerry?"

Noah managed his well-rehearsed niceties.

"God be praised. He is doing much better; his cancer has gone into remission since the last treatment; the doctor says No Stress!!"

Giggling nervously and fidgeting with her cardigan, Yolanda waved to Brent, the pastor in charge of outreach and the

Church offices. Once he passed, Yolanda resumed talking with Noah as if nothing had happened.

"So, I have been the perfect wife as always, of course. Jerry hasn't lifted a finger in weeks! I've even been surprising him with his favourite take-out every day! He'd be here, of course, because he is so thankful the Lord has saved his life, but missing his leg n' all, I told him to just rest. I set him up on his favourite recliner, and he has been catching up on all the pre-recorded shows on our satellite TV, so I am sure he is happy as a little piglet!" With a new burst of confidence, she continued: "How's your mother? She missed you today. She was disappointed you weren't at the outreach meeting this morning. *Very* unlike you, she said... *very* disappointed. Don't tell her I told you, but I think you do so much; taking a day off doesn't harm here n' there. I told her that you were wonderful and helpful, and we love having you lead our ministry!!!" Yolanda was full of empty compliments.

Thoughts started running rampant in Noah's near-exploding brain:

Poor Jerry, the only thing I'd regret if I were him was not getting faster-acting cancer to put me outta my misery sooner.

Compassion soon dwindled as memories triggered feelings of irritation:

Jerry is just as bad, always ratting me out to Mother when I was ever late to mass. I bet this is all Karma.

You are such a lying sack of manure, you crazy lady.

You'd just as soon trip me over train tracks to take my place. You're probably the one who told Mother I didn't attend the

meeting today. Knowing you, you called Mother just to tell her the news yourself!

Noah always thought his preferred responses to Yolanda, but they never made it past his closed lips. His thoughts continued; it made having to listen to her rubbish worth the seconds of wasted time:

Why couldn't it be Yolanda to lose her leg? At least Jerry is an honest asshole. Yolanda lies straight to your face, stabs you in the back at every chance she gets, and then demands an apology when you catch her being dishonest! Waterworks of a professional, tears on command! If being nasty was a super-power, she'd have it. I bet she collects the fears and screams of children in a jar, giving her strength to lie another day.

Noah began picturing Yolanda and Jerry in creepy villain costumes like you'd see in the old comics from the 80s.

"Well, see you next Saturday, Booth buddy!!! So excited to outreach with you!!! I have so much to learn; you are an inspiration to us all, Noah."

Yolanda placed her sweaty palm on Noah's shoulder.

"You are truly blessed to be such a wonderful instrument of the Lord and at such a young age! I will tell Jerry you sent your blessings. Tell your dear wonderful Mother, hello, and I'll see you both tomorrow, I'm sure."

"God Bless Yolanda, I am not feeling great, so I may not make it."

Noah did his best fake cough,

"I'll see you before Saturday if I am feeling better."

"Oh! You poor thing! Feel better soon! You wouldn't want to miss Saturday now!! It's supposed to be one of our biggest events yet!"

Yolanda said with a sneaky smile and raised an eyebrow.

Noah knew this meant she was up to no good, and he would regret whatever she did later, but he wasn't scared for the first time in his life. Not only that, it didn't seem to bother him near- ly as much as it used to; Noah felt strong.

"Yeah, wouldn't want that." Noah, mustering every ounce of energy he could just to pull out a half-hearted smile of false appreciation for her attempt at relaying concern for his actual well-being. Fed up, he quickly moved past Yolanda and prac- tically jogged back to the station wagon. Noah couldn't get back to his apartment fast enough to wash Yolanda's "essence" off his shoulder. Noah really had no interest in next Saturday's debacle and no interest in thinking about dealing with Mother when she realized he wasn't showing up to mass tomorrow. All he wanted to think about was Forgiveness Meetings, his new homeless friend Hank and what he would bring to his second ever Forgiveness Meeting the following morning.

He would just cross that uncomfortable bridge when he got to it.

UNCOMFORTABLE CHANGES:

PICK-NICK IN THE PARK

It was 10 o'clock the very next morning, Sunday. The day before, Noah had held his very first Forgiveness Meeting, and today was meant to be a promising repeat. He invited the homeless man from yesterday to re-join him and try a proper meeting this time.

Noah wasn't sure if Hank would even show up, but deep down, he was hopeful and looking forward to seeing him again. This time, the newly forming ritual began with a slight adjustment: Noah made a couple of to-go cups of coffee with a bit of sugar and milk, assuming all homeless people liked hot beverages. Then he toasted up a couple of his frozen breakfast sausage sandwiches to share and put it all in the temperature-appropriate compartments of his pick-nick basket gift he received last Christmas from Mother. At the time, he was disappointed with the inconsiderate flowery gift, but it ended up finding its use after all—all packed.

The thirteen random beach chairs and thirteen Forgiveness Meeting pamphlets [Yang the Master printer made him the day before] were already in the Jesus wagon. This time, Noah was going to park farther away, so people didn't stare at all the Bible verses plastered all over his vehicle.

Maybe nobody else showed up because they saw my car and thought I was a religious nut.

Today! Today is the day.

Today, people will flock to my meeting!

Feeling prepared and excited, Noah grabbed Prince William's leash, the pick-nick basket full of breakfast goodies, and headed out the door. What a great morning!! Noah was running a little late, but he was feeling so empowered he wasn't worried about the clock.

WHAT'S FOR YOU, WON'T PASS YOU BY

It was another beautiful day at the park. Street parking was gone, and the back parking lot was packed! Noah was headed out of the lot to check for street parking again when as if Jesus himself intervened, the exact same parking spot opened up right in front of him! "Damn it!" Noah didn't want the best spot again; he wanted to hide his beat-up religious billboard behind a wall or down the road a bit. He sat for a moment, idle. Thinking about what he should do, not wanting to park there, he checked the time, and it was 10:45 a.m. Still having to walk all the beach chairs in, he knew he'd be late if he succumbed to his embarrassment and tried to keep looking for parking. HOOONNNNKKKKKKKK!!!!!

"Hey, kid! Move it! Some of us have places to be!"

A large hairy man yelled out the rolled-down window of his multi-coloured El Camino. There was nowhere for Noah to go. He either pulled into the spot to deal with the dirty looks and laughter, or he sat there, causing a traffic jam. Another car was blocking the exit at this point, and Noah's boat of a Station Wagon wouldn't fit around that old lady's Cadillac even if he drove partially on the sidewalk.

"I'm sorry, Jesus. Thank you for the blessing."

But he wasn't thankful, not at all.

Noah's Father used to tell him:

"Son, the Lord works in mysterious ways, and whatever is for you won't go past you."

Then he heard his mother:

"The Lord provides Noah. Take what you're given and mind your manners!!!"

The engine was off, and Willie jumped out from his spot under the driver's seat and positioned his nose right where he knew the car door would open.

"Stay, Willie, let me get the chairs out to our spot first. I'll be right back." Noah pulled the random fold-up beach chairs out, stacked as many as he could manage on each arm, and set off for the ancient willow tree at the centre of the park. But by the time he got there, a massive group of BBQing, beer drinking, Frisbee throwing jocks, and cheerleading types had set up for the day, in HIS SPOT!!!

Where do I go now?

The meeting starts in five minutes, and I still have more stuff to get!

If I had only woken up earlier!

Damn it! I need this spot.

They look like they'll be here all day.

How is Hank gonna find me if I move?

Noah looked all around for an alternative meeting place. All the nice spots were taken. Stashing the beach chairs in a bush, he hurried back to his Highness. The windows were cracked, but it was starting to turn into a brutally hot day. Plus, Noah

knew he couldn't afford the fine for leaving his dog unattended in the car, and if Willie ended up in the pound waiting to die, he got passed up for adoption for being too old or too vocal. Noah would never forgive himself! So back he ran. His suit jacket peeled off, tie loosened and flapping in the air, and white button-down still buttoned to the neck.

Gosh, it's hot today

By the time Noah got within eyesight of the wagon, he could see the shape of a man putting his arm in the window. His dog looked happy enough. The closer he got, the more certain he was.

Hank? How'd he know that was my...?

"Hey, Pal. You're late! And you really shouldn't leave Pdub in the car like that. It's really hot out here; he could roast in this tin can of yours."

"Pdub?" Does Hank mean "PW?" I guess it's short for "P double u?"

Noah overthought pretty much everything.

"Yeah, sorry, I ran back as soon as I could. I was trying to bring some of the chairs to our spot. There are a ton of teenagers over there, and I'm not sure where to go now."

"Judging by yesterday's attendance, do you think you're gonna need all thirteen chairs today?" Hank chuckled and raised an eyebrow with a half grin.

A long pause as Noah unlocked the wagon to let his poor perspiring dog out. "I guess not..."

Noah found it hard to adjust to changes in thought, usually because he spent so long thinking about stuff. Noah grabbed the pick-nick basket and the pamphlets for the Meeting and hung his sweaty suit jacket on the back of the driver's seat. "Need the noose?"

Noah took Hank's advice, ditched the tie around his neck, and locked up the wagon.

"How'd you know this was my car, Hank?"

"You mean besides all the Bible verses plastered all over this thing, the yelping dog kinda gave it away. I heard the poor fella from across the park!"

"Well, I brought us some breakfast sandwiches and coffee for the Meeting today. Thought you might like..." As Noah reached into the basket, Hank cut him off with a smile:

"That's mighty kind of you to think of me and all, but I can't take any of that."

Noah's great morning just kept getting more and more disappointing.

"Did you already eat? I know it's hot, so maybe the coffee wasn't a good idea after all, but..." Noah looked defeated.

"No, it's not that. I don't drink caffeine; it's not good for my body. I'm a vegan and have been for years now. Tommy, the guy I play Mahjong with, got me into it."

A little irritated, Noah snapped unintentionally, "Aren't you a homeless alcoholic? Can you really afford to be picky? And isn't alcohol horrible for your body anyway? You're contradicting yourself. That makes no sense Hank." Realizing what he

said, he quickly apologized, "I'm an asshole, sorry. My filter is busted or something. I am really sorry, Hank. I didn't mean..."

"Yeah, you did mean it. It's alright; at least you're honest about being a dick." Hank laughed a hearty laugh. "And you are partly right, but I reason that being a vegan and an alcoholic balance out to giving me the average health of a thirty-year-old. So, I'm doin' alright. Also, it bothers me a great deal when you are late. If I can respect you for showing up, you can respect me for being on time. I don't have a home, but I do own a watch. If I can afford one of these and know how to tell time, so can you. You dig?"

Noah could tell Hank hadn't had a drink in the last twenty hours; his eyes were clear. He also didn't smell of piss and whiskey this time, which meant he must have had a shower and got new clothes somehow since yesterday. Continuing with his usual "beating himself up internally" sketch, Noah, scolded himself in silence:

God, why am I such an insensitive jerk? And why does he care about punctuality so much? I gotta be better about time management. Even a homeless guy is more on time than I am. Stupid, Stupid!

Noah started hitting himself on the forehead, scolding himself for his poor performance and behaviour. Hank softened his body language and changed his tone; the kid clearly had issues, too; no sense beating him up any more than he just did, "Come on." Hank gestured with his head, "I will show you another spot we can set up this Forgiveness Meeting; it's on the other side of the pond."

After putting the pick-nick basket back in the wagon, Noah, Hank, and the Prince of Willies headed back off in the direction of the partying teens to gather the hidden beach chairs Noah left in a bush.

"Sorry for assuming you'd eat whatever I brought you just 'cause you're homeless. And I shouldn't have been late regardless of my reasons. I guess that was a bit insensitive of me."

"I prefer the term 'houseless' actually; home is where your heart is, and don't worry about it, Noah. I'm sure there is plenty more than what meets the eye with you too. But as for being on time, I would really appreciate you working on that, bud." Hank took the leash off Prince William and threw a stick for the excitable hound dog, and continued off-topic:

"You'll love this new spot. Great view of some half-naked chick's sun-tanning!"

"I'm not here to check out women, Hank."

"I'm always here to check out the ladies. That's what eyes are for! Boy Noah, you don't get out women, do yah?" Hank yelled back, running for the prince, who was barking after a poodle who appeared to have a stunner of an owner.

"I guess not," Noah remarked, mostly to himself, then jogged awkwardly to follow.

FORGIVENESS CHALLENGE

Hank picked up the neon purple beach chair from the pile and plopped himself down after carefully choosing it. Then, without a care in the world, he stretched himself out; flinging off his flip-flops, Hank began happily absorbing the summer sun. Noah felt a bit jealous of Hank but couldn't pinpoint why.

"Sit down, Pal. Try relaxing a little bit; I promise it won't kill you, at least not right away. Take off those shoes you got on; the grass feels great on the feet."

Noah picked up the sparkly brown beach chair that was next in the pile and unfolded it with a horrible awkwardness, then proceeded to take off his shoes and socks methodically.

"Smell those feet? Whew! Damn! Haha, and you thought *my* smells were bad. So, how yah wanna start this thing, Pal? Is there some sort of a format?"

Trying to ignore the first part of what Hank said, Noah skipped straight to his response. "Well, I thought maybe we could read the first page or so of Forgiveness Meetings in the Book and then go from there..."

"Sounds good. Go ahead; I'm listening." Hank crossed his arms and placed his index finger to his mouth to emphasize theatrical thought, then closed his eyes and laid back like he was on vacation in the Bahamas.

Noah fumbled through his bag and pulled out the book.

"Forgiveness Meetings" Noah paused and looked up at Hank for approval, receiving not even a smirk.

"I'm listening. Keep goin', Pal. Need me to tell you to wipe your ass too?" Hank was having too much fun with this to let it slide.

So, the uptight perfectionist continued: "Forgiving and forgetting are two very different ideas. Even where forgetting is unfathomable, forgiveness is possible. Forgiveness is the healing ointment we dress our wounds with so we can continue on our paths towards more enlightened, happy, peaceful, loving lives." Noah paused and placed the book on his lap. He systematically began unbuttoning his dress shirt and rolling up his sleeves, sweat pouring from his face and underarms before continuing: "Forgiving our oppressors is NOT the same as forgetting what our oppressors have proven themselves capable of." Noah stopped and closed the book. "That isn't technically the end of the page, but I figured it was a better place to stop than mid-sentence. So, what do you think, Hank?"

"What do *I* think?" Hank replied.

Worried, he dropped into self-reflection and didn't hear every word.

Pause.

"I guess I think it all sounds nice on paper but forgiving someone who has treated you like shit isn't easy."

"Give an example" Noah began rolling up his best trousers as neatly as he could manage.

"Okay...well, for example, ummm. Alright, how about this: I walk by every morning past this French place, and there is this

really hot French bird smoking a cigarette that works there and might even own the place; she's there so early. Anyway, I walk by every morning, and I say 'another beautiful day,' and she hacks up her phlegm and spits it at me."

"Why the heck would you walk past there every morning if you know she is going to spit at you, Hank? That makes no sense."

"Cause she's hot." Hank smiled.

"And because there is usually food left out for me behind the Italian place, I have to walk past the French place just to get there." Hank sat up in the chair.

"Is there no other way to the Italian place? Why not walk the other way?"

"Because I go around back, and when you go behind down the alley, it dead ends at the Italian spot. So, there is no other way to go. At first, when she did it, I laughed at her, then I started skipping past her with a smile. Now I just say the same thing every time, 'another beautiful morning!' Somehow thinking maybe one day it might soften her up. No dice. She is still a cunt."

"Hank, the 'C' word is a bit strong, wouldn't you say...?" Noah interrupted.

"Well, she is one," Hank replied.

How does it all make you feel? "Noah Interrupted again.

"At first? Confused, hurt. But then it turned into a sort of embarrassment, followed by anger but now, I just don't give a shit. She's a cunt, and that's that. I have no interest in forgiving

her; she doesn't deserve it." Arms gruffly crossed like an ancient gnome.

Noah stopped to reflect.

"Can I suggest something? You might not like it."

"Do I have a choice?" Hank spoke with a clown-sized fake smile.

"Of course, you do," Noah said seriously.

"Then sure, yah, go ahead."

Noah looked up to the bright clear sky as he spoke.

"Well, forget about her for a minute. Since you don't care what she thinks anyway, what if... would you be willing to, each time you pass by her, and she spits at you; maybe say sincerely 'I forgive you,' and then just keep on walking." Noah surprised himself with that one.

"I never thought of that before." Hank toyed with the idea in his head for a minute. "Let me think about that one. Your turn. What do you think about the whole thing of forgiving your fellow assholes?"

Shrugging his shoulders in response. Noah had a hard time focusing on just one instance. "I have a number of things going on right now. A number of people that I resent or blame. But I keep pulling back to the idea that it's all my own fault."

"How so?"

"I just um... I just... I can't seem to figure out what I am even alive for anymore. I seem to be going with what the people

around me say is right even when I know in my soul that they are fucking crazy!"

"Fucking huh? A strong word for someone like you, don't you think?" Hank smirked.

"That's exactly what I mean! Why is the word 'fuck' going to send me to hell when there is stuff happening out there in the world that is way, waaaayyy worse!" Now Noah's blood was up.

"I mean, there is a politician and a tax guy coming to our church literally *selling* our congregation a talk for a few hours next Saturday for a thousand bucks. You'll never guess what for either! A talk on how to properly fill out your tax forms for the new 'carbon tax,' that is supposedly going to go straight to homeless Americans. I mean houseless Americans, sorry Hank."

"No worries. I understand. So where do you fit into all this?"

"Well, basically, they want ME to not only set the damn event up but also run the outreach booth with the wicked witch from God knows where and then tare the event down and do clean up while the rest of those ass holes kiss these two douche bag's asses to try and figure out how to avoid paying the tax, they spent the whole day promoting to the rest of us! I hate the whole thing! I don't think we should do the event, let alone PAY these guys, and all I could say to any of them was 'yah, no problem, see you Saturday.'"

Noah took a deep breath and sighed.

"So, I am pissed. More so at myself. I think what they are doing is wrong! That money won't make it in your hands, Hank. It's all just an excuse to bleed the population dry."

"Yeah. I could see why you would be upset with yourself. So, you are saying you want to forgive yourself? Or forgive the fucking morons puttin' on the show? Or who?"

"I guess all of the above."

"Well, I got an idea for you, and I don't think you will like it. Want to hear me out?"

"Sure, Hank."

"Okay. How about stickin' up for yourself and telling them all to shove their shitty little event up their asses."

"Hank, I can't do that!"

"Well, I can't forgive that French cunt."

Noah was winded; he wanted a change and help. That was why he started this Meeting in the first place. But how could he do what Hank was asking? He would lose his job! Hank sensed the dilemma, "I'm not saying to say it just like that; I am just simply saying for you to tell them you're not going to help. And make sure to tell 'em why."

Hank's eyes were crystal clear and intensely focused on Noah's.

Noah looked up.

"If I tell them I won't be there and tell them why, will you start forgiving the French woman every time you pass her? *Out loud AND* to her face, deal?"

"Deal."

Noah & Mother

BANG.

BANG.

BANG.

BANG.

BANG!!!

"NOAH!! OPEN THIS DOOR NOW!"

Looking over at his clock: 4:19 a.m.

"Mother is getting ridiculous now, Prince. Four in the morning? On a Monday?"

Noah groaned and threw his pillow across the room.

Then like a good little boy, Noah got up and put on his robe. His dog crawled back under the duvet; in moments like these, Noah wished he was a dog. He answered the door with frustration.

"Mother, do you know what time it is? It is four in the morning! I have a long day ahead of me. You cannot keep doing this! I am an adult! I know you don't think so, but I am! And you WILL stop pounding on my door at ridiculous night and morning hours. And you WILL start calling ahead before showing up! What if I had a guest?"

"At this hour? You better not, young man!"

Mother pushed through Noah's arm that blocked his door-way.

"Don't talk to your mother that way! You are a spoiled rotten child! I put this roof over your head, and I WILL take it from you if you EVER sass me again!"

No Boundaries. Ever.

Not sure if it was the time of day, the frustration from church events, or the new-found courage he got from his meeting the morning before with Hank, but it all just poured out of him:

"First, I PAY rent here, not you! Second, I am NOT a child! Third, if you show up at MY door before ten o'clock in the morning, unannounced, I will find ANY WOMAN AT ALL and make sure she's in my bed the next time you call! Is that clear?"

Mother tried to speak, but Noah cut her off;

"AND! If you EVER yell at me again, you will NEVER be invited in, and I will NEVER go to church with you again! Do you hear me? Father's the lucky one! I'd take his place in a heartbeat!"

Noah stopped. A moment of silence would normally be wel-comed but not this time. The mother began to cry. Without saying anything, she pushed past him and out the door, trying to slam it in his face, but his arm supported the door open.

"Mother, stop crying; I didn't mean that last bit. But come on! Four in the morning? I am not a child. I know how to work an alarm clock and a phone. I like your company, but be reason-able."

Noah reached to hug her, but she pulled back. Noah grabbed her and squeezed her, and shushed her to be calm.

"I love you, Mother. I am sorry I missed yesterday with you. I should have at least called you, but I didn't want you convincing me to go when I didn't want to. I didn't want you telling me what I was doing was unchristian, and I didn't want you doing exactly what you are doing right now."

"You make me sound like such a beast!" Mother spoke through her tears and relaxed in Noah's embrace.

"You're not a beast, Mother, but you can be a bit overbearing. You've done a great job, and I am doing okay. Alright? Are you okay? Want me to make you your special tea?"

Mother nodded and slowly walked to the kitchen table.

"You really hurt my feelings when you didn't show up yesterday. And Yolanda, bless her heart, called me the day before and told me how worried for you she was."

Unfiltered Thought:

Yolanda! I knew it. Super Satan!

Filtered Response:

"I heard."

Noah boiled the kettle and placed a Jasmine Tea bag in Mother's favourite mug of a pug.

"I know you won't like this. But I need to start speaking my truth, so I am going to tell you anyway. Let me finish before you start up with me, okay?"

"Well, Noah, you sh..."

"Mother."

"Okay, I promise."

Wondering where to start, Noah began at the end:

"I am starting up something called Forgiveness Meetings. I decided Saturday morning to try it out, and someone showed up. I wanted to keep the momentum, so I held the second one the very next day. That is why I missed church with you yesterday and the outreach meeting. I don't need a lecture, okay? I made a decision, and I am sticking with it."

Bracing himself for the shrilled screams.

"Noah, I think that's a great idea."

Mother smiled peacefully as she stood to pour the hot water into the teapot.

"Ever since your father died, I have been worried about you. You aren't the same happy Noah. You have zero friends, and it is sad. I have been showing up randomly, not for *my* health, but because I am so worried about you. You seem so fragile, angry, and lost. I don't know how to help you."

Noah stood up and gave Mother a hug, kissed her on the head, and took the teapot from her to pour her tea respectfully.

"I forgive you as I hope you forgive me, and I appreciate the effort. I am going to start making some changes in my life, though. You may not understand them or like them, but I have to do it, or I'm going to crack."

"Okay, just don't kill yourself. I know you, Noah, you're stubborn like your mother, but you have a soft heart just like your father. Promise me. I can deal with the rest."

"I promise." They both sipped their tea in silence for about ten minutes, but it felt like hours.

"So, are you excited about Saturday?"

"Well, that is one of those changes I am making. Mother, I don't agree with taxing people to breathe air, and I certainly don't agree with paying a politician and a taxman to come to the church for a political event. I am going to be bowing out of that. Don't be angry with me."

"Your opinion of me is so...I don't know, Noah. You don't really know me; maybe that is partially my fault. Noah, I love you, and I raised a good man. If you think that what they are doing is wrong, you stand up for yourself. I trust you. I am sorry if you don't see that."

Noah and Mother spent the rest of the morning watching the sun rise while they drank Mother's favourite tea. Silence never felt so good. Time flew by.

When things are good, there are never enough hours in a day. Moments you wished lasted lifetimes, only lasting literal moments in time. Time machine travel would best suit a morning such as this. Maybe, just maybe, it could find a way to repeat in the future. Why couldn't life just always be this nice?

THE FRENCH-IE

That same Monday morning on the other side of town, the second promise was being pondered. Hank woke up from his usual spot under the ancient willow tree in the park next to the pond. The exact same tree where he met Noah two days before. He pulled out the wipes that he bought on Sunday and began to wipe himself down. Dipping his head into the pond, he pulled out some bio-degradable conditioner and brushed it through his thick hair before sticking on his green beanie cap. Looking at his half-bottle of Jameson, Hank decided against it and slipped the liquid crutch into his camouflage print bag. Dressed in his "new" donation clothes, Hank started off toward his usual haunt: the Italian place.

It was still early, so Hank thought maybe that French broad wouldn't be around, and he could get out of having to forgive her. He was wrong. There she was, sitting on her black stool. Black fishnets, black glasses, black everything with her long-classic style cigarette not three centimetres away from her bright red lips.

Here we go.

Hank slowly started walking down the alley, looking straight ahead.

If she doesn't spit at me, then I don't have to forgive her.

Maybe, she decides not to, hopefully.

You can't forgive someone who doesn't do anything, right?

Approaching her spit radius, Hank tried to appear unbothered.

Hhhhcccccwachhhtu!

On my shoe?

Really???

Was that necessary?

Her aim has improved. Fuck.

Hank turned slowly and looked her dead square in the face. She took a drag from her cigarette and gave her nasty, raised-lipped, half smile.

Deep breath.

"I forgive you for spitting on my shoe."

Smirking, "I didn't ask for your forgiveness."

"I don't need your permission," Hank responded childishly, then turned and continued walking toward the Italian place.

The raspy French accent called after him, "Who do you think you are? Homeless Christ? Why don't you yell at me, slap me, and tell me what you really think?" She got up from her stool and began to follow him.

Hank put his bag in its usual spot near Mario's back door and bent down to pick up his neatly covered plate.

Damn, she's a sexy bitch. What a shame.

"You come here every morning to steal food from Mario, and if I wasn't here, you would steal from me too. You're the one that needs forgiving. Thief."

"Mario leaves this for me; he's an excellent chef. And for your information, I wouldn't touch that nasty French shit if you paid me to."

"My food is delicious. Why don't you get a job and stop living off the backs of others? Lazy slop."

"It's slob."

"Whah?"

"The word you are looking for is *slob,* not slop. Just so you know, for the future. Let me ask you something, do you get off on being a cunt, or is this just normal behaviour for you?"

"Hey, I worked my ass off to get where I am today, not to have some *slob* like you steal from my trash cans." Licking her conversational wounds.

"I'll have you know that once it's in the trash on public property, like this alleyway, it is no longer *yours,* Princess. So, it's not technically stealing, and secondly, and most importantly, I don't eat slop. I'm a vegan, not a pig."

"Uh! How would you know? You've never tried French cuisine!"

"Yeah, and if I'm lucky, I'll never have to."

Hank sat on his usual upside-down milk crate with a cushion, practically ignoring the woman at this point.

"How is it that just because you are American, you somehow feel entitled to everything? I worked my ass off to get what I have and to live here, and people like you... you just piss all over yourself and expect the Ritz!"

Finally realizing where she was coming from all those years, Hank saw jealousy! Taking a bite from his perfectly prepared plate, "God, this is sooo good. Mario's a true talent. You just don't get food like this on a regular ol' paycheck." Hank closed his eyes in ecstasy, rubbing it in just enough to even the scoreboard a little.

"Don't you feel the least bit guilty? All my taxes are taken out to fund bums like you!" striking her high-top table in frustration.

"I have you know that I paid good money in my previous life to be able to afford myself this lifestyle. You assume a lot of things about me, lady. The truth is, you don't know a damn thing, and you never took the time to ask either; you just spit at me every day for five fucking years. And that makes you somehow better than me? Blow your smoke in someone else's face. I've earned my peace, not that I should have to. Everyone has a right to live how they wanna live. At least here we do! So why does what I do bother you so fucking much? Are you jealous?"

"I am most certainly not!" She pouted.

"You know why Mario leaves me food back here every morning for the last five years? Do you? Have you ever even bothered to ask the man?" Hank relaxed.

The French bird popped off her high-top chair and started walking over to him, shaking her head no as she sat on the second milk carton, lighting her second cigarette of the morning.

"I used to come into Mario's every day for twenty years. The first time I met Mario, I was much younger and had just finished University. I had shown promise and had even won awards for my designs. Mario was a friend of my father's, and he asked me to design him a restaurant. So, at the age of twenty, fresh out of school, I designed him the nicest place at that time. Mario was ecstatic that everyone had come to his spot. And I mean everyone who was anyone. I made that fucker popular, let me tell you. So, that is why he leaves me food."

"You're a liar. That makes no sense."

"In fact, I designed this whole block. I can tell you every square foot of your own restaurant."

"Prove it." French flirtation slowly peeked out behind her rough exterior.

"Okay, ask me anything." Hank took another bite of his cold sautéed string beans.

"Where is my walk-in storage room?" She challenged.

"Trick question, you don't have one. That grey box was originally a real estate office. You have to store your shit in the basement I designed for the last owner who loved collecting wine."

"How did you know that?" She resounded in disbelief.

"I told you, and I don't care if you believe me or not." Hank felt more confident and took a bite of his salad.

"Then if you're some hot shot architect, what are you doing homeless smelling of booze and piss most mornings?" The woman exploded angrily.

"Uh, Uh. My turn to ask a question. What makes you think it is okay to spit at someone every day, year after year? Was that taught to you as a kid or something?"

"No, it was not taught to me. My parents died when I was four. I was raised by my grandpapa, Pierre. He was a great man. He'd be tossing in his grave if he knew I did that." She laughed to herself. "So, what's the deal? You answer my question first now."

"I killed my wife and newborn in a fire. They were sleeping in the house I built. I was out of town on business designing a building for a Japanese tech manufacturing mogul."

"You weren't there. How did *you* kill them?" Her eyes started to fill with tears for her unexpected new friend.

"Your turn."

"The first time I spit on you was because I had a horrific night the day before, and I wanted to take it out on someone. You were there, so it was you." She lit her third cigarette. "You laughed at me and danced off, which made me laugh. It made me feel better."

"Okay, but why keep doing it then?"

She raised her eyebrows, signalling his turn.

"I killed her because I was cocky. I used solar panels before they were safety checked and didn't properly wire the electrical system; I thought I knew it all. Well, apparently, she turned on the heating in the house, and it somehow caused a short; I think it had something to do with how I hooked up the gas and the lines crossed. A spark is all it takes, you know? Anyway, the solar panels were an electrical fire; fire trucks came at record

speed, but they had no idea about the solar panels. Not sure if you know, but water and electrical fires don't mix; they were dead before the firemen could get inside. They were outside with their arms crossed, doing nothing. What could they do? And me? I was in Japan. I should have been the one to die. Not them."

"But I don't understand. Why are you homeless?"

"Houseless."

"Okay, 'houseless.' Why? You can still work, can you not?" She was resolute and demanding.

"Cut the crap. Why do you continue to spit on me?" Hank needed to know.

"I spit on you because I can. After the first, I did it a second time to see if you would react. You just skipped on passed." Shugging. "After a while, you just ignored me. I began to wonder to myself, why does this man do nothing? Why does he not spit back or yell or chase me inside? Then, after a while, it just became ritual. Today there was something different. You didn't smell of piss and booze. I aimed right at your shoe and wanted to see what changed. Maybe I am a cunt, as you say; I don't care anymore. Dealing with assholes all day, all night, I just don't know why I bother or fight for this life anymore." Her tone seemed to change, and she sounded almost human, almost. With a deep heavy sigh, she looked down in defeat.

Hank acquiesced. "To answer your question, I left Japan immediately and went to what was left of my home to bury my young wife and child. I tried sleeping in beds after that, but I just couldn't. Do you know what it is like to have nightmares every night for five years of your loved ones burning alive in a home you built? I killed my family. I don't deserve to be com-fortable. Anyway, Mario feels sorry for me, so that's the story in a nutshell." Hank finished his plate. He wiped it clean, stood up, and neatly placed it on his seat.

"I promise I won't spit at you anymore if you promise me something."

"What."

"Try a plate of my food tonight. I will make sure it's vegan. Let's say dusk." Flirting again.

"I don't eat slop, remember." Hank smiled.

"Ha, ha, very funny. I'm being serious." Slowly batting her eyelids.

"So am I."

Hank started to walk away, "God sees the truth but waits."

"Tolstoy." The French bird responded with a pleasant sur-prise.

"Dusk it is then." Hank, without turning around, smiled at her unexpected depth. He wasn't sure he would go, but it was a nice thought.

A DEAL IS A DEAL

"Soooo Pal, how'd it go for you with the church freaks?" Hank was delighted with himself.

"Honestly? Not great. I didn't lose my job because Mother promised them that her sizable annual donation wouldn't be made if a certain someone was fired, and by certain someone, she meant me."

"What the fuck happened?" Hank belly-laughed.

Exasperated, Noah started.

"Where should I begin? Yesterday, after my mother came barging in at four in the morning and we had a blow-out, I went into the church offices to find Brent, the Pastor in charge of Outreach."

Noah took off his tie and threw it on the ground.

"And...?"

"And what do you think happened?" His eyes grew wide.

"I told Brent I couldn't participate in Saturday's event, and I wasn't going to man the booth for Outreach."

"What did the bastard do?"

"He flipped! He didn't even hear why. So, I forced it on him and told him I didn't agree with paying people of the state more money for a few hours than they do out of the entire month feeding the houseless. He said if I didn't do it, I would no lon-

ger be in charge of Outreach, and they would no longer need my help during Wednesday night meetings. I was shocked! It was flowing from his lips like he'd been waiting years for this moment! I explained that in the Bible, there was even a story of Jesus himself angered by the people in Temple of his day doing business in the house of the Lord."

"What'd he say to that?"

"He said Jesus would want his flock to be informed and prepared; and that the tax was going to the homeless, which meant the tax was doing the Lord's work. Then he said if I didn't support the Lord's work, I might be tempted by the devil himself, and I needed to step down. Then came the kicker! He said he wanted to give the Outreach leader position to Yolanda! I fucking hate that woman! Everything she touches turns to shit."

Noah leaned forward in his beach chair, head in his hands, the Prince of Willie's jumping up into his face trying to console his human.

"Whoa, there, cowboy! Don't fly off your horse just yet! Take a breather."

Speaking through his fingers: "I think I'm going to have to start looking for another way to make money. I don't think they want me."

"That's it? I dislike the institution of religion just as much as the next humanist atheist, but giving up because you think your fellow religious nutbags don't WANT you there? Correct me if I'm wrong here, pal, but I don't believe this chick wrote about Forgiveness Meetings as an excuse for people to give up."

"But...I..."

"But, you, what? If I have to forgive my fellow assholes like that camel at the French place, so do you. The meeting adjourned till Thursday. Same time, the same place. And I want results outa you kid." Hank got up, folded his chair, and carried it off with him.

Noah didn't move a muscle.

Forgiving these people is not going to be easy.

The self-righteous rarely feel the need to be forgiven for their misgiving, doesn't Hank know?

They don't have any! So, what's to forgive?

Noah really didn't want to have to do what he was being asked to do, but a deal is a deal, and surprisingly enough, Hank held up his end of the bargain with ease.

Noah's Turn.

A Truth's Many Sides

Noah woke up to knocking at his door. It was Mother again.

"Noah. I don't have much time."

"Just open the door, Mother. I am in the kitchen." Shuffling to the kitchen mid-sentence. Noah couldn't get the coffee poured fast enough.

"What have I told you about locking your doors?"

An impatient look fell upon his face.

"Noah. I received a call from Brent. He told me what had happened. That you are not interested in doing the Lord's work; raising money for the homeless."

"Houseless Mother, not homeless. And Brent told you HIS version of what happened."

"Regardless," she responded, "I told him in not so uncertain terms that if your job were given to anyone else, my contributions would find their way to another parish's coffers. You WILL have to continue going to the meetings for the events, but Brent will run the event set up and tear down himself from start to finish. They will expect your presence at tonight's meeting. I have to go; lock your door!" Door slams.

Noah's sigh of relief was almost as loud.

Prince William let out a whimper and started his morning pee-pee dance. So, without a second thought, Noah attached his leash and walked out the front door, leaving it wide open after him. When they arrived back, nothing had gone missing, and no one had let themselves in uninvited. He was a little bummed out because, deep down, having less stuff was starting to appeal to him.

Noah spent the rest of his morning psyching himself up for the meeting that evening and thinking of what to say and do and possible attitudes and responses he would receive from the others. Shaking and chattering teeth; if it wasn't springtime, Noah would have just grabbed another jacket, but it was too hot out for that, and he knew he'd look crazier in a jacket than with chattering teeth. With a few hours left till he had to go to church, Noah drove to Yang for someone to talk to. Yang had a soothing way of calming the nerves.

He was like an energy bath; you could say anything to Yang, and it was okay.

VIRGIN DRAG

"Hey, Noah. You look horrible." Yang was never one for social niceties.

"I'm so nervous, Yang. I'm literally shaking. This is so ridiculous. I promised Hank, the guy I do my Forgiveness Meetings with, that I'd forgive the people in the church, but I'm so worried about what they'll say and do. It's just stupid."

"Yeah. I'm tired of people's bullshit. I care lots like you before. Now I just smoke grass. It's legal, so no biggie. It calms my nerves. Slow me down so I think properly. Helpful. Not for everyone. But make some people paranoid, and a few go nuts-o."

Yang twirled his finger around his right ear as he crossed his eyes. Noah laughed in a slightly nervous manner.

"What do you think it would do to me, Yang?"

"Your Mother will not like it."

Yang shook his head with eyes wide, yet Noah sensed that Yang did not disapprove.

"I know. She dislikes ninety-nine point nine percent of what I do."

"People call it a gateway drug. I am not the reason you loopy on smack or dopy on the poppy flower."

"Yang. I'm not that adventurous. This is a big enough deal as is. I don't even drink and am not interested in looking like a pimple-face tweaker or a dead-man walking Skeletor. All I do know is that I can't function like this. My teeth are chattering, and it is a million degrees outside. I just want to calm myself long enough to deal with these people at work without losing my backbone, my job, or my cool."

The desperation in Noah's eyes was hard to fake. Yang was not impressed.

"Well, if you lose your job, I hire you. I need an assistant I trust anyway. You definitely fired after this one." Yang laughed.

Pulling out what looked like a hand-rolled cigarette, he continued: "I leave out back near recycling. If it goes missing," Yang shrugged his shoulders and went out back.

Noah, not fully understanding the stoner customs, waited about five minutes before following him out, but Yang was nowhere to be found; however, the doobie was right where it was meant to be. Noah reached for it, still shaking from nerves, took the lighter that was strategically placed next to his personal joint, and firmly pushed his thumb down over the metal-ridged wheel. It was one of those decorative Bic lighters that said 'Kiss Me I'm Irish' and was covered in shamrocks. Noah laughed. Putting the perfectly rolled paper to his lips, he used his left hand to cover the other end of the joint to block the wind, and with his right, he made fire. After the first virgin drag, he felt nothing.

So naturally, he puffed and puffed till he coughed and sent the whole world tumbling down around him like a ton of bricks

he had been carrying unnecessarily for far too long. Time stood still. He thought he must have been in that alleyway for hours.

Getting a little worried someone might see him, Noah thought about leaving. Deep down, he knew it didn't matter if someone did see him, but decided to get going anyway. Putting out the remainder of the joint to save for another time, Noah began his evening's mission.

This particular walk to church was long overdue. He had given Yang his keys and felt confident that he was parked in a spot that was not metered. He despised parking meters. He despised most things that cost unnecessarily large amounts of money for no good reason. So, he avoided parking meters as much as he could and suffered through the rest.

This was the first time Noah ever walked to work. The first time Noah ever went to work stoned. Heck! It was the first time Noah was ever stoned, period! And minus the tiny bits of paranoia he got randomly, he kinda loved it!

The only thing he regretted that day was that it had taken him this long to try it. He didn't plan on doing it every day, but he was sure as hell not against trying it again sometime.

He continued his walk to the church, having the most wonderfully engaging thoughts and conversations within his own head about anything his ingénue brain could think up.

Noah thought about how beautiful the world looked around him, how he would like to try more steps in the book, and even thought about what Mother would be like if she were stoned.

This made him smile because he pictured her being fun and happy.

He imagined what it would be like if he ever was able to meet the woman who wrote the book. Would he even recognize her? What would he say if he did? Was she a nice person? What did she think the world would end up like if everyone on the planet took her book to heart and did all the steps the way she saw them being done?

Then the church came into full view, and Noah began to worry he would start to shake again, but magically he didn't.

He was calm as the Cheshire cat, possibly as Mad as the Hatter, but he was damn certain he was still as quick as the White Rabbit but with the added bravery of Alice to take on the wicked nameless "they" [as are present in most fairy tales and children's novels]. Noah wasn't scared, he wasn't tongue-tied, and he definitely wasn't going to humour any of their bull-shit. Instead, Noah was resolute.

Random thoughts continued as he approached the campus of the church.

What would all these people be like if they followed the book?

Would this concept of religion and the attachments we have to superfluous things and all the random rules just fall to the waist side?

Would the politics that we know today be necessary or even useful?

Would people be nice? Honest? Trustworthy? Reliable?

What if everyone all at once decided to stop being self-ish-egotistical assholes?

The last thought made Noah laugh. He knew he'd never see the day, at least not at the destructive pace humankind had managed to speed it up to, regrettably. He knew they were all doomed; it was all just a matter of time. As sad as that was, it didn't make it any less true for Noah. He just couldn't picture a world where everyone was nice, helpful, trustworthy, reliable, fair, and happy without being slaves to money, people, or time. If he wasn't stoned, that last thought might have depressed him. Instead, it just made him shrug and positively wonder if the book could somehow change all that.

CLEAR CONSCIOUS CONFIDENCE

"Hey, Noah." Randy came over from the bench he was sitting at with a hot new nineteen-year-old girl. Randy met her at a college-age church mixer, his favourite place to pick up chicks. As into her as he was, Randy could see something was different about Noah, and he was determined to figure out what it was.

Noah gave Randy a half-hearted smile while still looking at the ground as he made his way to bent Brent's office. Randy trotted to catch up with him.

"Hey, Noah, wait up!" Out of breath due to his fast-food lazy lifestyle, Randy grabbed Noah's arm to slow him down.

"I think I'm in love with this one; she's a ten out of ten and a good Christian girl. I was thinking, I'd..." Randy caught a whiff of Noah and leaned in to get a better smell.

DEEEEP Inhale.

"Whew! Noah. You smell like a skunk! Were you in the woods? Or rollin' in some stanky grass?"

Randy looked Noah dead square in the eyes, excited for the drama.

"You're high, aren't you?!"

Noah's raised eyebrow and his case of the fuck; it's written all over his face said it all.

Randy stood back, disappointed and disapproving.

Shaking his head with his "I will pray for you, brother" look on his face. Noah wasn't interested in self-righteous-judgmental "forgiveness" anymore.

"We can pray later, Randy. Right now, I'm on important business."

"Go home, brother. You don't want anyone to see you like this. You're a mess."

Now Noah was offended. "Actually, that's exactly what I want. I'm tired of pretending what's going on in this place is the Lord's work when it has nothing to do with the Lord."

"What do you mean?"

"You know what I mean. A politician? A tax man? Come on, Randy, I know you are not stupid. What about any of that seems right to you?"

"We're helping people Noah. The money's going to the homeless."

"Houseless."

"What?"

"HOUSE-less. Home is where your heart is, Randy." Noah finished awkwardly.

Noah took a deep relaxed breath. "Look, Randy. It doesn't matter. Forget it. I just don't belong here anymore."

"Of course, you do, bud!"

"No. I don't. I don't even know why I'm alive."

"You are alive to do the Lord's work, Noah."

"Okay, Randy. And what *is* that exactly? Turn all non-Christians into Christians? Save the world from sin and evil?" Noah stopped walking and faced Randy. "Look, Randy. I'm twenty-five years old, and I am already tired. Tired of everything. It is all fluff, and nothing makes sense to me anymore. I spent years trying so hard to be perfect. To tell you the truth, I have no clue what the fuck that even means."

Randy was about to correct Noah on his choice of language, but Noah put his palm calmly and firmly up while shaking his head as if to say, "Don't bother."

"Randy, I love you, man. I deeply care for humanity and call this planet home just like billions of others, but I am so tired of playing these bullshit societal games that get me nowhere. Can you honestly tell me you are happy, healthy, and wealthy? Can you look me in the eye and tell me you love your life as it is? Cause I can't. I am miserable and tired of caring so much while others go around undoing all my hard work with a single selfish-greedy decision or three."

"What are you talking about, Noah?"

"Forget it; I'm talking nonsense. I gotta go. All I know is something has to change, or I'm gonna crack. All this hypocritical—selectively self-righteous, religious stuff isn't working for me anymore. Maybe I'll see you around sometime. Good luck with that girl. I hope you find happiness there."

"That's it? Man, you don't give up on God just because a handful of people think paying for a seminar to help people is worth using our tithe money on. It's going to the homeless!"

Noah knew arguing was futile.

"Okay, Randy. But just so you know, I'm not giving up on God. There's a better way to help humanity, and I'm not gonna be able to do it sitting in meetings and booths. Take care of yourself. Good luck." Noah gave Randy a heartfelt hug and started walking toward bent Brent's office, leaving him stunned at what just transpired.

By the time Noah got there, he could hear Yolanda's giggle coming from Brent's office. He could smell their nasty greasy lunch; everything about them was like nails on a chalkboard for Noah.

Tap Tap Tap.

Noah's middle finger's knuckle against the hardwood door was louder than expected.

"Come in and welcome visitor."

Noah could hear the flirtatious undertones in bent Brent's voice.

"Hi, Brent, Yolanda. This won't take long. I just came to inform you I won't be at tonight's meeting or any meeting. You two get what you want, after all. And you know what? I'm not the least bit angry. I was disappointed at first, mainly because I thought you all had sense and backbone, but I don't care anymore. You have your own crosses to bear.

And I forgive you, both of you. I forgive you for your ulterior motives, your unchristian behaviours, and your weird relationship, which I am sure your wife and husband would not fully approve of. I don't want to work with you people anymore. You do more harm than good, and I want no part in any of it.

I forgive you, and I bless you away from me. You can mail me my final paycheck."

Without waiting for any response, Noah closed Brent's door peacefully and then walked back to Yang's, feeling the most confident and free he'd ever felt in his whole life. A huge hypo-critical weight had lifted off his shoulders, and he couldn't stop smiling.

He officially had no job. He had no money for rent or bills.

He had no clue what came next.

But what Noah did have was something money couldn't buy him:

A clear conscience and a feeling of freedom, only forgiveness could manifest.

Goodbye lies, deceit, and fake niceties; Hello integrity and unlimited possibilities.

R.E.S.P.E.C.T

Noah walked home to get the prince of hounds with nowhere to be and nothing to do. Willie was clearly excited about a walk, and even he could tell something was different about his human companion. Seeing how his mental flight was beginning to feel a bit too grounded for his liking, the cloudy euphoria now resembled more of a clear-skied desert. Noah decided he'd walk back to Yang's to finish what he started out back in the alley. When Noah reached his destination, he could see Yang in his weathered wooden chair, smoking, as usual. It was a funny thought, but Noah couldn't recall any moment seeing Yang outside without something lit in his hand.

The familiar scene made Noah feel at home. Yang didn't know it, but Noah began smoking cigarettes years ago because he wanted to be like Yang. Yang always looked like he had life figured out; he knew who he was and what he wanted. If mimicry was the sincerest form of flattery, then Yang should have considered himself flattered. Truth be told, Yang never knew Noah looked up to him or that he wanted to be like him. Yang was just nice to Noah and always treated him like he was a man, even when Noah was just knee-high to a grasshopper.

Sometimes that's all that's needed to make a difference in another's life. A little bit of respect goes a long way regardless of age, sex, creed, or colour. Noah pulled out the half-smoked joint and handed it to Yang, who lit it and passed it back after his two puffs.

Noah smiled and followed suit.

Yang spoke first: "So I'll see you tomorrow at eight in the morning. I have a big project. Prince can come to stay while you help me."

Yang knew by Noah's demeanour that he was not planning on returning to the church any time soon, which meant he would need a job ASAP.

Noah nodded and reflected on Yang's kindness.

The two men shared Noah's moment of freedom and peace in silence and with dignity.

Uncomfortable Changes never felt better.

Clearing some preconceived notions, people, and things from his life, was a painful necessity Noah was beginning to steadily embrace. But little did he know, the uncomfortable feelings and even more uncomfortable decision-making were far from over.

Step by step.

Bit by bit.

Noah was changing his world.

Pain never felt so pleasurable.

And thus, the night continued: Puff. Puff. Pass.

THE GOLDEN RULE

Noah woke up with a smile from the best sleep he could ever remember having. It was 6 a.m., and he was refreshed and ready to start his first day at Yang's. Expectations were low; excitement was high. What a beautiful day! He knew he would have to break away for a quick meeting with Hank seeing how Thursday was, but Noah didn't think this would be a deal breaker for Yang.

Yang understands what I'm doing and why. Yang even has his own copy of the book! He will be okay, won't he? Yes, He must.

Noah; is still overthinking every last detail.

On to the next mental struggle: Not knowing what to bring, he just packed lunch for himself and his dog and made sure to dress in his cleanest button-down shirt and slacks. Mother always told him it was better to be overdressed than under-dressed. That was a lesson he fully agreed with. He hated being underdressed. He would rather have all eyes on him because he looked too good than being looked like an inconsiderate and ignorant man who didn't belong. Whether or not that is what people thought, it was what Noah was programmed to believe true as a general rule.

It was now 7 a.m.

Noah was ready to go and decided to walk. It was healthier, cheaper, and less stressful than driving all the time. In fact, it was at this moment our dear Noah decided to himself he would change his driving to a walking quotient and try reducing his

driving down to twenty-three percent and increase his walking to about fifty percent, leaving the remaining percentages to public transportation, riding a bicycle and the likes. It would have been twenty percent, but Noah knew he wasn't perfect and needed at least a three percent margin for error, like super cold days, lazy days, and the occasional sick days.

By the time his unnecessary transportation percentages had worked themselves out in his head, he had tuned back into his reality and saw how close he was to his first day of work.

Excited and nervous:

What a day to be alive.

What a life to be living.

He wondered to himself what his friend would think of his accomplishment. Hank was sure to have opinions. Thoughts were interrupted by greetings. Yang handed Noah a coffee and a small white paper bag filled with not one but two of his favourite doughnuts! A deep sigh and smile were Noah's version of a thank you that morning, and Yang was fine with that. Friendship tends to be a funny thing. Your friendship transcends socially demanded behaviour and rests in telepathic understanding. There is a sense of comfort in knowing that even when you don't act as you are told to communicate your point properly.

Yang broke the silence.

"I see the prince is happy. I set up an area for him out back."

Noah was beginning to suspect Yang had hired him for his dog. Willie had a way with everyone. If animals could speak in the human tongue, Prince William would be an easy-to-love

Chris Farley or Chris Rock [listed: death before beauty], and Noah would be Woody Allen, an acquired taste at best.

"Okay, here is the project I need you to bind, one for each student. I will print and put it together properly. All you do is use this machine and punch through the holes. Then you grab like this and push spiral trough. I have special plastic wax I will show you to put on the sharp ends of the spiral. Safer for kids; Touch!"

Yang pulled from his back pocket and pushed into Noah's free hand his example of a finished book for him to feel. Yang was right; instead of just pushing in the sharp end bits of the spiral, a quick dip in that waxy stuff seemed like a great idea for the youngsters.

The two men and their trusted mascot got to work. Prince William had a giant toy to tear apart, and this one seemed to be made of recycled carpet, much tougher than his usual soft plush toy. Ripping out the eyes and nose would take hours of dedicated tearing and gnawing, and the prince took this job quite seriously. After Noah started to get the hang of his task, his alarm went off.

"Yang, I gotta run out for about an hour to meet Hank for a scheduled Forgiveness Meeting. He hates when I'm late."

"Call him. Tell him you're busy."

"I would, except that Hank doesn't have a phone."

"Who has no phone anymore? What is he? Homeless?"

Yang chuckled at his seemingly harmless joke. Noah stared blankly at Yang.

"Oh. Gotcha. Okay. Do you mind staying longer so we finish tonight?"

"No problem at all. Be back real soon."

"Hey, Noah."

"Yeah?"

"Hank friend, right?"

Noah nodded yes.

"Why is he still houseless if you have a house?"

It was clearly a rhetorical question seeing as how Yang spun back around to continue his task at hand with no interest in an out-loud response.

That stung Noah's pride a little.

He put his shoes back on as he reached the front door and started his walk to the park. He struggled with the idea that the right thing to do would put him at a disadvantage and in a position of weakness. He didn't know Hank wouldn't steal all his stuff. He loved his stuff, all of his stuff. Even the stuff he forgot he had or could not find or misplaced for safekeeping. He didn't know Hank wouldn't ruin his place. He didn't own his place; it wasn't his to ruin. It was a risk. But to calculate that risk, he would have to consider more than just his feelings and judgmental thoughts. Noah would have to consider what the right and humane thing to do was; he would have to take into account the Golden Rule of treating others the way he would want to be treated. And then he would have to make a decision that could [and most likely would] disrupt the fabric of his entire existence.

Was he willing to do that?

Did he have a choice?

Just because Yang said that didn't mean he had to do what Yang suggested. But was what Yang was suggesting the RIGHT thing to do for him and for Hank?

Deep down, Noah really wasn't sure.

By the time he got to the Park and saw Hank already there in a lotus pose under the Willow tree, he decided to think about it. So, taking off his shoes and sitting quietly facing Hank, he did just that; think.

After what seemed like an eternity, Noah could hear Hank stirring.

"Noah. So, how'd it go, pal?" Hank spoke softly as his eyes slowly opened.

Noah, wide-eyed and in deep thought, was brought back to reality.

"Not sure how to explain it. I got a new job. I guess that sort of answers that question. I just could not do it anymore, Hank. I felt like a slimy hypocrite just being there. I got stoned at Yang's, walked to the church yesterday, and felt liberated. I felt strong, Hank. I knew at that moment that I would never step foot in those offices to work again. It didn't matter if I had to join you here in the park; does that make sense?"

Hank nodded.

"Yang offered me a job before I left, but I wasn't sure if he was just being nice or if he really meant it. Turned out he was

serious, and I started this morning. I'm learning how to spiral bind. I'm not saving the world or anything, but I feel better making school books than I ever did at the church."

"You are saving the world more by binding school books than you ever did, bashing people over the head with a religious textbook that was written thousands of years ago to control the population. But I digress, my friend. The only way to save this world is through unbiased learning and teaching. But you know what, Noah? That seems to be a basic idea that we as an entire human race haven't quite seemed to grasp yet. If you really think about it, pal, we should be teaching our future generations about finding new planets in new galaxies to populate for the time when our planet doesn't make it through a fatal asteroid hit or the inevitable galaxy collision with Andromeda, our next closest galaxy in the universe. So, if you really think about it, Noah. You are saving the world with every book you bind. And don't you ever forget that."

"That's not religious, though; that is science, Hank."

"From a religious context, who do you think made all the science-y stuff? Everything that science describes and prescribes? How we use our tools determines if it is "good" or "evil." God doesn't say, "Pray and do nothing! And all will be given to you." You have to put in the work like AA always says at the end of each meeting: It works if you work it, and you're worth it! Know what I mean? So, the sheer fact that we even know asteroids and other planets exist is our gift from this God of yours to do something about it, don't you think?"

At that exact moment, it clicked; Noah had his answer.

"Hank, would you like to move in with me? You are my friend, and I like having you around. You make sense, and I would be honoured at the opportunity to share my apartment with you. It's not big or anything, but it does its job."

Hank looked up at the sky and thought deeply about his beautiful young family, and something clicked in his own mind. His wife's memory deserved respect and love, not feelings of guilt, regret, and fear. He needed to face these feelings. A night indoors was a good way to test himself.

"I might take you up on that for a night and how it goes. But I promise nothing." He gruffed.

"Great! How about this, you walk me back to work, so you know where it is, and then meet me there when I'm done. We can walk back to the apartment together."

"I accept your kindness, but you have to know something; I have a hard time indoors, so if I don't stay, don't take it too personally, pal."

"I kinda figured that after you told me your story, Hank. I would have asked you sooner, but I still had hang-ups about what I was told to believe about houseless people. Yang helped me work through that one earlier today. You'd like Yang."

Noah stood up and dusted off his butt. There was a clinical awkwardness about him and the way he talked. Like, it was as though he thought if he didn't thoroughly explain himself, then people wouldn't understand him at all.

"Where's all your stuff, Hank? I can help you carry some of it, and we can pick up the rest later when we get the wagon. I

walked to work today. I'm sure leaving your stuff at the shop wouldn't be a big deal."

"This is it." Hank reached around to the side of the Willow tree and grabbed his backpack with his yoga mat attached to the top with a bungee cord. Everything neat. Everything tidy. Like all of Hank's thoughts and feelings, everything in its place and pocket is neatly compartmentalized.

The walk back to Yang's printing shop appeared peaceful to those who passed by, but in each of their minds, a whirlwind of fears and expectations spun faster and faster with every step closer to their new lives of living together.

ONE MAN'S TRAGEDY

Noah walked into the shop with ease as Hank stayed outside uncomfortably. Hank avoided the front door of most shops due to the unwelcoming nature of most folks found inside them.

"Yang! I brought someone for you to meet!"

Noah spun around and saw Hank still outside, unable to cross the imaginary threshold line. Noah quickly half-jogged back and grabbed Hank by the forearm, leading him in without a second thought. If Hank were a small child learning how to swim, Noah would have been the adult tossing him haphazardly into the deep end without questioning his ability to sort it out mentally.

Yang came out from the back room with a big smile and arms in the air, welcoming Hank like a congressman would, and prepared for a photo op-scheduled embrace.

"Hank! I hear loads about you. Welcome. Come in, come in. I have a nice couch back here. Leave your bag. Relax, Relax. Come in."

Yang had his arm around Hank's shoulder, guiding him in toward the back room.

Hank took a deep breath and exhaled.

It was nice to be treated like a human being again. Hank had almost forgotten what that actually felt like. It wasn't enough to exist. It wasn't enough to eat, drink, sleep, shit, and breathe on

this planet. It was being treated nicely. He was feeling another human's touch without fear of pain. It was something every living being on this rock deserved but rarely received.

It was overwhelming. If Hank didn't actively work to keep his usual calm, collected, hard exterior, he could feel himself releasing emotion in a million different directions; one of which involved the universal sign of male weakness: tears.

"Yang, how long have you been here?" Hank was digging deep, trying to place Yang in a history of faces locked in his psyche.

"Ahhh...About two decades or so." Yang started to chuckle at his age.

"Do you remember a woman named Mama Yin? She lived here around seven years ago, had an acupuncture and herbalist place just next door to here...?"

"Yeah. Dragon woman! My ex-wife! Why? You know her too? I apologize." Yang chuckled.

"Yeah, she was my acupuncturist in my past life."

"You look familiar; what is your family name?"

"Farmopolis." Hank plopped himself down on the brown corduroy two-seater couch positioned perfectly in the centre of the room.

Yang laughed as he poured the rest of his morning coffee down the small sink in the corner near the back door. "You know architect, dude? His name is the same as you; funny name hard to forget." Flipping the tab on the electric kettle, Yang looked in its reflection to see Hank's reaction. He knew exactly

who Hank was from the moment he first heard Noah speak of him. Small towns get much smaller where drama is concerned. Everyone likes a good story, especially when death is the head-liner.

Hank lifted his eyebrow with interest.

"Poor guy lost the whole family. Fire. Crazy stuff. Life is so precious. I read on paper. It was around the time my ex was sucking all the blood from my bank account." Yang started to laugh uncontrollably and then continued.

"Jealous, so jealous. I wanted to trade spots. Funny. Tragedy, for one. Blessing for another." Yang kept laughing, then turned to face him square on.

"Yeah, I knew him." Hank understood.

"Change is scary. Only if you learn nothing from it." Yang wasn't laughing any longer.

Noah was sooooooo confused. He was crouched against the wall behind Hank across from Yang. Prince William was curled up on his lap, enjoying an ear rub.

It was always fascinating to Noah that pressure points in the ears managed to reduce stress. Mother would rub his ears in between her thumb and index finger while he lay on her lap as a child, watching shows late at night when Father was working late or away on business with the church. It was the closest he ever felt with Mother. He found that repeating this ritual with his dog was just as relaxing.

Noah's train of random thoughts was interrupted. Hank and Yang were walking out back, each with a mug in their hands.

He left the two men and continued his work spiral-binding the books. He really enjoyed his new job. Noah never thought he would be more excited to continue working than to go outside to hang out with his friends in a million years.

But there he was, happy, productive, and at peace with his new vocation.

FREE CYCLING & FREE MARKETING:

MR. GQ

It happened by convenience that Yang's printing shop became the new meeting place of their Forgiveness Meetings. Every so often, the three men would work on a printing project while they conducted their meetings; the authentic experience contributed to the success of their time together each week. Working together was like a social meditation, creating an organic space for open, honest communication.

On one such occasion, Yang was mid-rant when the doorbell rang. Yang's brain was so focused on getting his points across that a plane could have crashed next door, and that still wouldn't have registered. Being a good portion of the way into why he no longer did course at the local Scientology Mission, Yang could not control his emotions; tears were welling up, fixin' to pour like the flooded Shannon River. He loved the courses and missed the satisfactory feelings that came with completing them. Yang missed the people and the way he was treated like he belonged. He was confused why the prices couldn't be lower or on a suggested donation basis for those who didn't have the money. Yang believed the courses on ethical, moral, and logical thinking were important and valuable but not for the sake of bankrupting the middle and lower classes. He knew money didn't buy happiness, but it sure did help with the basics.

Yang had gotten to the part of his rant where his wife was leaving him because the church told her in no uncertain terms she would be asked to leave too if she continued to be in contact with Yang, her husband. The door jingling and slamming finally interrupted Yang's pain, anger, and agony enough to prevent a potential mental breakdown or heart attack.

A very well-dressed man walked into the back room before Yang had a chance to control himself properly. Laughing at the state of Yang, the man plopped down on his couch facing the three men collating hundreds of pages of legal documents for the local law office.

"Hey, Yang, my brother! How are you feeling these days?" The man's laugh was even comfortably upper-class.

Ali was a jolly GQ sort of gentleman. Any lady he happened to glance at was putty in his hands. Being content with his partner and having no intention of exploring other sexual opportunities, Ali never took advantage of the swooning Bella Donna. Ali's partner was the yin to his very clearly distinguished Yang. Love? The unconditional sort. Ali went to school with Yang when they were younger. After graduation, Ali was told his massive inheritance hinged upon him moving back to his family's home country. So, like a good Muslim son, he obeyed. In University, he desperately tried to find the opposite sex attractive but nature appeared to be winning the battle over nurture in his case.

"What are your feathers all ruffled up for?" Ali had a wonderful twinkle in his eye whenever controversy arose that didn't directly involve himself. He called drama the "brain candy of our foremothers" before soap operas came along, took all our good-old-fashioned fun, and locked it in a boob tube.

A colourful man, Ali was: a New York-born and bred aristocratic Mother; daughter of a banker and a fashion designer. Saudi Arabian born and bred aristocratic Father; son of an oil mogul and a Princess. After so many years, Yang took a beat to process Ali's presence in his shop. Yang was trying to remember the last time he saw Ali; maybe it was years ago at their high school reunion. Now, here Ali was sitting on the couch like it was yesterday. They used to spend most of their youth on that same couch. Playing the old Atari games with their dinosaur PCs set up on the old coffee table that Yang's father found them at a swap meet, years had flown by and dusted over with foggy idealistic memories of their youth.

"Long time no see, champ. Where is Ahmed?"

"Probably praying for my soul. Sometimes out of pure boredom, I join him, but mostly my frustration prevents that from being a regular occurrence." Ali laughed his hearty laugh, then continued, "Why are you so out of balance, old friend?" He knew just how to speak to Yang. Immediately Yang relaxed his clenched fists, and his tightened neck and shoulders plopped down next to his friend and brother from another mother taking, exhaling as he fell.

Yang passed Ali the Book from their coffee table and spoke softly: "Forgiveness Meeting. First Section."

"Yeah, I read that on the plane ride over here. I am not sure a few points would work, but her intentions seem pure. So what? You three started a meeting, didn't you? Not a bad idea. Can I sit in? I am interested only if what I think she was saying and what you think she is saying are similar. Ahmed especially liked the third step, but I am content to start at the beginning. He keeps trying to convince me to set one up with him; the free-market thing I told him that is doing things out of order. Plus, I sell Clothes, so why would I set up a free market? Sounds like sales suicide."

Ali was always the OCD realist. Order and timing, and of course: PROFIT!

He didn't get his sexuality from his father, but he sure did get his work ethic and stubbornness. His laugh, though, was his beautiful mother's.

"It wouldn't be for your new designer clothes unless your old season was haunting you like a bad ex-boyfriend. It would be for people like Noah here." Hank went straight in for the kill to make a point.

"Why me?" Perplexed, Noah, still collating away like a good worker bee, barely looked up yet was fully engaged in the conversation just the same. A.D.D. definitely had its perks.

"Because you are a hoarder, and even if you attempted to sell all you're shit online, no one would buy it all. That's why you." Hank billowed.

Male pride stung; Noah retaliated before his filter could properly kick in, "What would you know about having stuff? You can't even keep a roof over your head!"

"No one understands the pain of letting go more than I do. But holding on to all that shit ain't gonna bring your daddy back, pal."

Noah stopped working and walked out back in search of a roach. Yang attempted to get up to follow him, but Ali stopped him with his arm as Hank stopped him with his eyes.

The only thing harder than feeling pain and loss yourself is watching the ones you love feeling it. Hank and Ali understood this, yet they both also knew these were the type of feelings that needed to be felt to invoke and inspire change. Suppressing or blocking them just prolonged the whole process doing no favours for anyone involved.

It was silly, holding onto so much stuff that there was barely room to walk. But what was sillier was watching a loved one do so to the point of self-destruction without saying something and offering a helping hand, and Hank was never one for being silly.

Hank and Ali connected in thought as though they had known one another lifetimes before. Enabling and ignoring were no longer good enough for their new friend Noah and Yang was too close to the situation to help properly.

Ali finally understood that free marketing and freecycling had nothing to do with economic espionage. It was about healing and reconnecting with the outside world. Ali was so attached to his self-centred thoughts and motives that he failed to see all the reasons that had nothing to do with him.

Hank raised his eyebrows and signalled to the back door, where Noah sat smoking himself back to sanity.

Ali nodded back, "I'll call Ahmed."

INTERVENTION FOR NOAH

"Another day in Paradise, huh, boys?"

Hank had a way of always making an entrance. Prince William was Hank's new bestie. He bought him a new collar and leash that said "Bad to the Bone" and had silver rounded spikes between each. It had been a week since the first mention of Noah's hoarding, and not a word had been spoken about it. When Hank wasn't walking The Dub of dogs or playing his coveted games of mahjong, he was now filling the rest of his time at Ali & Ahmed's place, organizing an event that would change the course of history forever. On this day, Hank was sent on a mission by Ahmed to recruit Noah and his mountainous stacks of stuff.

"Noah. I'm working on a project, and I need your help."

"What is it, Hank." Noah didn't really care to know, but the social obligation of politeness forced him to respond.

"I need to have a meeting at the apartment."

"What kind of meeting."

"A Forgiveness Meeting."

"Why can't you do it here, Hank?"

"Because the only time my friend is free is later at night, and I told him all about the meetings, and he wants to meet you first. I've unfortunately painted you up like some forgiveness meeting guru. He won't leave me alone about it. What do you think, pal? Favour for a friend?"

Noah nodded.

Little did he know the favour was for himself, and his physical world was about to be turned upside down.

"When Hank?"

"Tonight, at ten o'clock. I gotta go. See you then!" Hank pulled Willie's leash and headed out the front door of the printing shop, winking at Yang as Yang passed with coffees heading in from his daily doughnut run.

"How is Hank today?"

"He's just come by to ask me for a favour. He wants to have a meeting at the house tonight. He must think I'm stupid."

"Why." It wasn't really a question. Yang and Noah had subconsciously already had this discussion. Out loud was more for formality's sake.

"Because I know it has something to do with getting rid of all my stuff. But I won't do it, Yang. All my stuff is valuable and useful. What if I need it, but I gave it all away? I would just have to buy it again."

"Need what?" Challenged Yang.

"I dunno. Any of it! It's all useful stuff. And any of my books will go over my dead body!"

"Books are different; no one is trying to take all your books. But come on, Noah, when was the last time you used your elephant bed sheets?"

"When I was fourteen. But when I have a kid, they can use them."

"What if the kid is scared of an elephant or like a pony instead?" Yang smiled.

"What are you getting at Yang?"

"Stuff is stuff. Getting easier. What if you are offered a great job in Africa or the Philippians? You can't take with you all that. Expensive postage. Cost too much."

"I don't plan on moving to Africa or the Philippians. I like my apartment."

"You miss my point."

Yang ushered Noah outback and lit a joint as he opened the back door.

"Noah Keeping stuff won't bring him back. It only holds you back. Do you still have a drum set?"

"Yeah."

"When did you last play?"

"With my dad."

"When?" Yang pushed.

"When I was ten."

"What if a boy out there who really wanted to play the drum but can't afford it and you have a drum rotting in your closet? What if you give away at free-market and boy find, play, and become next Ringo Star?"

"Ringo Star?"

"Now, imagine you keep set till you die. The boy never gets it. The boy ends up working at fast food GMO Junk Land, gains 500 pounds, and dies at 30."

"Are you accusing me of murder, Yang?"

"No." Yang took another drag.

"I accuse you of ignorance, fear, and laziness. You could lose it all in fire, and then what? Wasted! Stuff is meant to move. Shared stuff better. Stuff needs attention and love too."

"It's just stuff, Yang, not a real living thing."

"Life is what you give it."

"I give life to the printer. Ali gives life to clothes. Ahmed gives life to pictures. Hank gives life to mahjong set." They both laughed. Noah finished the joint and followed Yang inside. "I could go into energy equalling light and mass and how everything is one and the same, but let us stick to the basics; what you give life to is Up to you, Noah. You give life to books. You have too much stuff rotting in stacks. Let someone else find value and give life."

The two men worked in silence the rest of the day—each in their own mindful thoughts.

Yang made his points, but letting go wasn't just about the stuff for Noah. It was about the memories attached to it all.

YOU'RE NEVER TOO YOUNG FOR BAGGAGE

Earlier that same day, Ahmed had shown up early. It was about 10 a.m., and Hank was already back from the print shop categorizing and separating Noah's belongings. After clearing out the living room, the sorting began. It was a week of meeting secretly at Ali & Ahmed's place, and now it was D-DAY, the day of deliverance from stuff. Whether Noah knew it or not, he was the key to the whole experiment. And if you really sat down and thought about it, that's all any of this was: A giant social experiment.

"So, how did Noah take it?" Ahmed went straight into helping sort through the Elephant tchotchkes, occasionally stopping to take pictures of it all.

"He's suspicious, but he said okay. Hopefully, Yang sorts Noah out and can convince him. Now, all we gotta do is hold up our end. Just leave all the books. If we touch those, it's game over. Ready?"

Hank felt like he was in a cheesy 1980s Movie.

"Yes, books are sacred; I will just organize them on shelves here. Better than hundreds of floor stacks. By the way, Ali knows a woman who gets us a spot in the park for the whole day. And I have social media talking. Should we make a flyer and sign for the town?"

"I dunno. I don't think printing all that is ecologically friendly and probably goes against this whole recycling idea. Maybe just a sign outta recycled stuff we find."

"Do you want a coffee? I need one before I start tackling the next mountain of shit."

The two men laughed to the point of tears. It was so much stuff making it a virtually impossible task ahead of them.

"Hank. I look at this and think how much easier it was to explain information systems to Ali. And that was no easy task, I tell you."

"Was."

"How much easier it *was*. Thank you. I get those mixed a lot."

"No problem. I wrote a paper back at the university years ago and was at it for the whole night. It got to me so bad I forgot how to spell the word "world." It just didn't look right. It was then I knew I needed a break, and I also needed to stop procrastinating till the night before the due date."

As the two very different men progressed through the piles upon piles of random stuff, their laughter filled the air. Noah's hoards managed to bring two people of seemingly completely opposite views and life stories together.

It was a mission to save their friend from his own self-perpetuating insanity.

Taking them eleven hours, only breaking for prayer and decaffeinated tea, and then stopped.

"Are we done?"

"As done as we're gonna be."

Hank dusted off his thighs and stood up after hours on the floor. His legs felt like tingly jelly.

"I feel good, Hank. Once we got started, it felt like mediation."

Hank looked up at the tops of all their categorized piles in disbelief. He really couldn't believe they got through it all.

"I can't believe Noah lives like this. He's too young to have this much baggage," Ahmed remarked sympathetically.

"You're never too young for baggage, Ahmed. You clearly haven't met his mother."

Ahmed collapsed on the couch next to Willie, his new old friend, deflating while patting the pooch on the head, "I know. I know. Meet anyone's parents. Parents try so hard or not at all. Some even try to destroy their children out of jealousy or social pressures. It is all such madness. When you know this, I wonder why I am not like Noah with loads of comfort collections. My father stoned my mother to death because she was raped by his own brother, who lived with us. So, I know this idea of baggage."

Before Hank even had a moment to process what Ali had said to him and respond at all, they both heard footsteps, and then the door handle moved.

Noah was home.

Strange.

What seems harsh to others feels normal for those who live these harsh realities. And Ahmed's reality was no harsher than Hank's if lives were swapped. Both lost love to death and tortured themselves, believing they could somehow have prevented it if given another chance.

There was a sameness in their difference. And they both had come such a long way.

VEGAN DONUTS

Emotions, smells, colours, feelings, and even tactile memories of the moment carry on through eternity long after the talking and listening about it cease. These are the moments tattooed on the soul and known to change the course of an individual's history and thus the history of humankind. Noah mentally prepared himself for a discussion; he was nowhere near ready to process what he saw in his living room that Wednesday evening. Up until that moment, he was confident he could still wiggle out of the Uncomfortable Change requested of him. His life of impulse purchases, gifts kept out of guilt or perceived future necessity, the stuff his dad left him as well as every birthday card or a bit of wrapping paper he'd neatly kept for years. It was all on display in his living room in chronological order, no less.

Noah dropped to his knees.

Hank and Ahmed stood, anticipating a meltdown.

All Noah could muster were three words spoken from the core of all his memories past:

"It's all there."

"Pal. Just know we love you, man. You're not alone in your madness. And because of you, I'm not alone with mine."

"Hank helped Ali and me go through our stuff. We would be honoured if you would do Free Market with us. You are not your stuff, just the same as we are not ours."

Noah's eyes began to water. "No, but all my memories are. I can't let go of him. He would never forgive me."

"Your dad wants nothing but happiness for you. If an old pair of his runners and newspapers dating back fifty years are holding you back, then all your father's efforts and love would be wasted, no?"

"It's my job to keep it all alive." Noah let his tears fall unashamed.

Hank thought carefully, then spoke compassionately, "Okay," clearing his throat, "Pal, why don't we bring the newspapers to the library to start? That way, you can see them whenever you want."

Noah looked up at all the newspapers, sat back on his ankles, and fought the illogical attachment and irrational emotions as best he could.

"I love my dad."

"We know."

"Keeping all his stuff won't bring him back. I tried before myself."

Noah asked the question *Who?* with his eyes.

"My mother." Ahmed knelt beside Noah.

"How old were you?"

"Nine." Noah was filled with shame.

"It's okay. I was just as attached as you are. I was forced to let it all go when a bomb exploded near my house. I was away at university at the time. Luckily my uncle, father, and his whore weren't."

"Whore is a pretty strong word."

It was like an involuntary tick; Noah could not help himself.

"A day after my mother was murdered, that woman moved in. I found out later she knew what my father was doing, and she helped him."

"Why?"

"Mercy killing is less shameful than divorce, I guess. To tell you the truth, the only thing I wish I had saved was my mother's old jewellery box that my grandfather handmade for her when she was little. I see you as lucky, Noah. All that I had was ripped from me. You can choose to let him go peacefully. You can watch his memories find new homes. I envy this. I selfishly wish to be there why you do so that I can experience just a moment of it for myself."

Noah stood up, walked through the maze of material shackles, and decided.

"So, when do we do this?"

"Tomorrow, I have one of Ali's trucks coming to pick all of it up for us."

"Fine, but I want to bring all my dad's stuff there myself."

Hank finally spoke up while handing Noah a small box.

"We found these in all your stuff. Sometimes the most powerful reminders are the smallest ones."

Inside were Noah's father's cufflinks, tie clip, and money clip. Noah remembered when his mom took him to the art fair street market to get them. Noah thought they were the coolest things he'd ever seen. They were mostly black with silver squares, all uniquely designed, reminding Noah of the aurora borealis.

If tears were left, they would have flooded with appreciation for his friends.

Little things are big things.

And this was quite tiny in a huge sort of way.

"Alright, pal. We have a busy day tomorrow. I think we ought to call it a night. That okay with you, Ahmed?"

"I couldn't agree more. Be here to start loading at five in the morning. I bring vegan doughnuts."

"That can't be tasty."

"Yee of small faith. Religion has the opposite effect of its aim. This is exactly why I don't go to the mosque anymore. The highest concentration of hypocrites."

"You stopped to pray at least a hundred times today. What do you mean by 'not religious?'"

"I pray to Allah, my Allah, my loving, compassionate, and just Allah. I do not worship men or giant boxes in the sand. Those are just means of population control like your churches or the temples of the Jewish community. Yes. Some good has come from groups of people working together for good. However, I have seen first-hand the bad that group-think can do. My views of Allah are peaceful, powerful, and loving; he who

asks me to do what is right. I can only do what is good and right if I think for myself.

If I allowed other men's interpretations to control my relationship with Allah, I would be a very sad, confused, angry, self-hating gay man."

Ahmed grabbed his coat and finished his thought, "Plus, these texts were written way before our time for people way before our time. If you take it all literally, it will send us all back to the Stone Age. Do you agree, Hank?"

Noah cut in, "I understand perfectly, and I love my God. My God is good. If I just blindly kept following the people in my church, I would be marched right off a cliff and into politics!"

The three men laughed and adjourned for the evening. There was a lot of unspoken agreement. Tonight's friendship had no class level, religious foundation, racial connotation, or sexual orientation.

It was peaceful and understanding as friendships and as all humanity should aim to be.

PENNY LOAFERS

Noah found himself pulling up to the park and slipping into his same trusty parking spot. His Jesus wagon was packed with all of his dad's stuff. It had been a while since he drove his wagon with Willie under his feet, snug as a bug for a trip to the park for adventurous sniffing and tree marking. It didn't seem to bother him anymore. Before, he was proud and loud about the Bible verses on his vehicle. Then he was embarrassed and ashamed. Today, Noah was at peace about it. It was what it was.

When Noah turned the engine off, another decision was made; Noah decided to use this opportunity to cleanse himself. Like a snake shedding his already dead layer of skin cells to make room for new healthier cell growth, so was Noah making room for his new healthy growth. It was dawning on him slowly, like a happy waking child, that his uncomfortable changes weren't just about himself anymore. Examples were being set, and it was time to step up to the plate to take a good honest swing so others could release themselves from their own debilitating fears.

Prince William was excited. A living creature's intuition can be so spot-on it's eerie. Noah knew he wasn't feeling it off himself because Noah wasn't excited, only resolute, solid in his choice. No, it was clearly felt from somewhere else but from where? Noah got out of his wagon in his dad's old favourite shoes, still one size too small like all the rest. He didn't care if

it didn't match the Bahama shorts and Hawaiian shirt. This day wasn't about other people's opinions.

Prince William jumped out and started pounding his front two paws on Noah's knee. Noah was busy trying to decide what to take out first, so the prince, not content with being ignored, took off running, galloping, tongue out and off to one side, ears flopping about. Noah slammed his door shut and ran like a madman in pursuit. The more he ran, the more in focus the willow tree became. It looked like a massive party and picnic! A giant banner made out of recycled cans spelled out.

"Free-Market"

Noah stopped running when he saw Willie's leash grabbed by Yang. He could hear the music and smell the food. All he could think about was how amazing it was to see all the people practically filling half the park. It was an overwhelming feeling of love and happiness Noah had never felt before. He wanted to bottle this moment and wear it on his sleeve-like cherished cologne whenever he wanted to feel good again.

Without planning his next five courses of action [another first for Noah], he sat down Indian-style on the grassy carpet below his feet and took off his father's old favourite shoes.

Sitting as straight as he could, breathing as deep as he could, and smiling uncontrollably: The sight was majestic to all those who passed by. Noah didn't care about how he looked; he was just happy. He was in love with this moment and had to soak up as much from his senses as he could manage before it inevitably ended, as all moments do. Eyes closed; Noah meditated for the first time.

Not the slightest clue how long he'd been there, eventually, he came back to reality nice and slow. First, moving all his toes and then every muscle till his eyes finally opened. Noah could feel the presence of someone beside him for ages but movement at that time to fill curiosities addiction was out of the question till he forgot they were even there. He thought it was just one person and assumed it was Hank. When Noah's eyes opened, he stretched slowly and looked around to see twenty-two people all sitting around him with their eyes closed; smiles plastered on their faces of varying degrees. Trying to be as quietly courteous as they all were to him, Noah stood up softly, leaving his shoes intentionally behind.

MAHJONG TOMMY

What a magnificent day. As he approached the giant "Free Market" sign made of recyclables, he could see something different between the cans. Upon closer inspection, hundreds of elephants were made out of paper and fabric.

Staring in disbelief and trying to make out where he'd seen those exact elephants before a strong hand landed on his left shoulder.

"Hey, Noah. What do you think? Ahmed and I found one of your old sheets. It had watermarks, so we cut it up for the sign." Noah recalled his old sheets fondly.

Ahmed continued, "Did you see all your stuff?"

Noah remembered he had loads still in his wagon and was about to bee-line it back, but Hank knew exactly what his young friend was thinking and stopped him mid-escape.

"Noah. We already grabbed the stuff from your Christ mobile. Relax and check this place out, Pal. It's amazing! I recommend starting with your own free stuff; Ahmed is there waiting for you." "Do you know where Willie went off to?"

"Ha-ha. Yeah, all the ladies in the park are taking turns minding him. Studly McPrince. Dude's getting more action than a Young Elvis." Everything was taken care of and thought about. This was true friendship. "I think I will go to my booth last if that's okay. I want to check everyone else out. I know what my stuff looks like already, so I know I'm not missing anything."

Hank nodded and headed off in another direction. "Enjoy!"

The first booth was massive! It was practically a mansion's worth of stuff packed into a small, randomly shaped space. Noah assumed it was a bunch of people's stuff all crammed together until he saw Ali chilling in the broken-down Forgiveness Meeting beach chair, wearing elephant glasses. Noah's dad bought him those at the zoo. Noah just couldn't avoid his own booth, could he? A great, unmistakable sign that is spelled out in recycled bits and bobs:

"Noah's Freedom"

There was an empty beach chair next to Ali that he signalled for Noah to sit in. Noah was flabbergasted by how much he had been living with, crammed on top of him for so many years. Overwhelming, to say the least.

"Ali"

"Yeah"

"You are aware that your chair is the broken one."

"I am aware it *was* the broken one, but not aware that it currently still is."

Ali's mischievous look told Noah that this particular conversation would take work, and Noah just wasn't that interested.

"Ahmed will be back shortly."

"Have you been here long, Ali?"

"No, not really, just brought Ahmed food from the other side of the Free Market. I set up a booth of last season's clothes,

and next to me is a lady giving away pita with falafel. It's Ahmed's second favourite food."

"What's his first favourite?"

"Vegetable Biryani."

"I would not have guessed that one." Noah smiled. There was so much he didn't know about his friends.

"Ah, look! My love! Hey, Ahmed, I got you this."

Ali stood up to give Ahmed back his seat, giving Noah a chance to sneak a peek at the newly fixed rump rest. It looked as though he took an old seat belt and tightly connected each end to the two sidebars.

"Looks good, guys."

Ahmed came over for a hug, so Noah stood up out of consideration for this friendly gesture trying not to be the awkward penguin that he was.

"You like? Old seat belt, fabric stapler, and really strong rubber glue. I have been using it all day with no issues!" Ahmed was very happy to see Noah.

"I saw you meditating on the hill."

Ali could see he was no longer needed and took this as his conversational queue to head back to his booth. He left his two beach chair bums as they resettled on their Thrones.

"Yeah, I thought Hank had joined me, but it turned out a load of randomers had me surrounded by the time I woke up." Noah wriggled.

Noah glanced around and continued, "Has anything been taken yet?"

"You mean 'Free-Cycled?'" Ahmed laughed, "Actually, yeah, almost one-third! It has been very nice to experience. Everyone is so confused and uptight when they first approach, but by the time they leave, they are happy and relaxed. I assume this is part of the process. I am quite enjoying it. That's why I am staying here. I like to watch people, and some let me take their picture." Ahmed continued to talk as he showed Noah some of the pictures of the different people and the items they finally chose to keep, "I tell them what the market is about, and I tell them about you and about why we are all here. Then I sit back and watch their change."

Ahmed could see out of the corner of his eye an older man walking into the Free Market and came over to eye one of Noah's father's suits.

"Take what you like. If they don't fit, give them away to another. Welcome to our Free Market; my name is Ahmed."

The older man was still clearly very confused. "I don't have anything to give you for these suits. I only have bus fare on me."

Noah chimed in, "Well, it's a good thing that all of it is free then. Take them. In fact, take all of them if you like." Arms stretched out like a circus presenter.

The older man was still skeptical. Ahmed turned to Noah and quietly whispered:

"This is where the man asks us where we got all this." Ahmed chuckled, delighted with himself.

"Those were my father's old suits. I've been hoarding all this stuff thinking it will bring him back. But it is time I let the stuff go. It's just collecting dust and making my asthma flair up. Those suits are better off with someone who will love and wear them. There are shoes too if they fit."

The older man's furry white-haired eyebrows raised compassionately. He was reminded of the time his father passed all those years ago, and how attached he was to all of the hats; realizing he was wearing one such hat, he took it off his head and handed it to Noah.

"I'll only take your father's suits if you take my father's hat. You know, my father demanded to be turned to ash and sprinkled over the ocean somewhere beautiful. He didn't want us attached to a tombstone. I hated him for that for years. But then I got a job in Europe to help build that Paris amusement park, and I understood. No matter where I was in the world, so was my father. I've been at peace ever since."

At that very moment, Noah found the old man's hat was now part of his "Uniform." Something to always cherish and commemorate this day.

Looking around at all the stuff while he spoke, he settled on three things: Two suits and a plush bean-bag elephant toy.

"My grandbaby will love this. Thank you, boys. Good luck with all this here. You're doing well." The old man let Ahmed take his picture and then walked off. Smile, suit, and be as happy as a raffle winner.

"Wow. So that's why you're still sitting here."

Ahmed smiled.

"Well, it looks like you have this under control, so I think I am going to check the rest of this place out if you don't mind." Noah took one last look around.

"Oh, of course. If you pass by the book and cookie lady, could you grab me a vegan cookie? Hank said they are delicious."

"Sure, by the way, where is Hank?"

"Mahjong."

Noah busted out laughing, "No way! Where?"

"His friend Tommy is teaching kids how to play, so Hank is helping."

"That's really nice of them. When you first said Mahjong, I just assumed he left to go play. That's why I laughed."

"I understand. Have you ever played?"

"No."

"Don't knock it till you try it."

Noah felt like a scolded child but accepted the criticism like a man.

"You know you're right. Maybe I will see if they can teach me the basics."

"Good. Then you can teach them to me!"

Laughter was a good theme for their Free Market Day.

Noah started walking, noticing he was still barefoot, he turned to ask another question, but Ahmed had spotted fresh

Free Market meat by that point and was already giving them the well-practiced tutorial.

Noah walked on; he would sort it all out eventually himself.

EPICURUS & THE FLOWER CHILD

The next booth was that of an artist. The woman was painting a bicycle.

"Is the bicycle for Free-Market?"

"Well, I need it to get home with all my art bits if there are any leftover. I won't be able to carry it all on foot the distance I will be traveling. But, if it all goes, by some miracle, sure. Only if you promise to use it, she needs love."

The woman smiled. The beauty from her youth transcended her wrinkles and long flowing black and grey hair. She was fit, and she was feisty. Noah was entranced.

"Don't you have a car?" Noah poached.

"Nah."

Noah changed the subject, "How long have you been doing this kind of art?"

"For a while now. I used to be an insurance salesperson, but my conscience kept eating away at me. Plus, it didn't seem like one day could pass me by without my friend in the claims department telling me horror stories of how she routinely had to screw customers over, so the company didn't have to lose its billion-dollar profit margin. It was making me physically ill."

"So, I still don't see why you ended up making art."

"Art is awareness; this is my way of making people aware of the power of giving, forgiving, and healthy non-GMO diets. Working in an insurance office, I felt that burying my head in the sand for a paycheck wasn't worth the heart attack. I read everything I could get my hands on. I found out that if we all reduced our consumption by at least twenty percent, ate healthy, clean food, ate way less meat and animal products, and stopped stressing ourselves out daily, cancer and most illnesses would greatly reduce in our population. As would the need for all the stabby jabbies and such."

"Stabby, what?"

Noah thought she was talking crazy. Cancer was only cured by radiation or cutting cancer cells out. People just got it and dealt with it. And what the hell was a stabby jabby?

"You know, Stabby Jabbies vaccines and all that. I mean, what is this immune system for if not for building up immunity? Ha! Silly Fear-riddled Leaders. Always claiming faith, yet having none of it themselves."

He could tell she was just getting warmed up, and mixed feelings were brewing inside of him as to whether he should make his offer or not. Maybe she was a religious nut like he used to be. Did he really want his car going to a person like that? A person like him?

She examined his face carefully, "What's your name if you don't mind me asking?"

"Noah. What's yours?"

"Marigold."

"Like the flower."

"Yep, exactly. My mother always called me her flower child. Perceptive woman, right?" Marigold laughed.

"Sorry, Noah. I get really passionate about all this. I just know deep down that if the world got together and treated our enemies, families, and friends all just a little gentler and kinder, we could sort all our disasters and dooms out without extortion, war, genocide, and eventual total annihilation."

Marigold picked up a keychain she had made and showed it to Noah. "This is my keychain I designed myself. It is a picture of the world I believe is possible." Noah smiled and showed her his.

"Mine is what I thought the world was all about. My dad gave it to me."

Marigold wore decades of hurt, sadness, and love on her face as she looked at the keys and chain of Noah's past, her future.

"I understand more than you know. I was a Catholic in my day."

"Born-again Christian." Noah raised his hand for his own call of attendance.

"So, Noah. What are you doing with yourself these days?"

"I am working at a printing shop, working through 'a book' and attempting to find meaning and purpose to my life."

Marigold busted up stitches in laughter.

"Aren't we all?" Curious, she poached: "What book?"

"It's called 'a book'. It is sort of self-help in the beginning, but it morphs into solutions for larger parts of your life and society.

It is taking over most of my thoughts these days. I find myself intoxicated by her optimism. Of all the years of me going to church and religious functions, I never once felt the way I do now reading her words."

"Must be interesting. Is it a cultish book? I'm not judging, just wondering."

Now Noah was the one laughing, "I don't think so. I think it was just a book written by a fellow apathetic and frustrated human being who believes it could all be so much better. She is an idealist, like you."

Marigold smiled and said, "I'd love for you to come by sometime. You can check out *Epicurus* and maybe bring this book you're talking about."

Noah dug a little deeper, poaching again, "So you're not far from here then if you ride your bicycle. How long does it take you to get to... Ummm, *Epicurus*?"

"About three hours on the bike from here, but it's much closer by car, so don't worry."

"Is *Epicurus* your address?"

"No. It's just the name of our community. *Epicurus* was the father of all communes, a Greek philosopher that studied under Aristotle. He decided everyone should live happy lives and that people were happiest when surrounded by friends. Then Epicurus moved all his good friends in and lived the rest of his days totally happy. Eventually, the idea spread like wildfire because it was awesome, and loads of communes were set up all over Europe and the Middle East. Unfortunately, the crusades came around, and all those happy, cooperative friends

were kicked out to make way for all the self-loathing monks; monasteries were originally communes, you know! Religion is so peaceful, isn't it?" She said morbidly

They both chuckled together. "Wow."

"Yeah!" Marigold was wise beyond her current lifetime. You could just tell.

"Well, Marigold. I would love to see Epicurus. I'll remember to bring the book." Noah looked at her, still debating. "So, if you give all your art away and finish your bicycle in time, you will just give it to me?"

"Yep, of course."

"Then how will you get home?"

"Walk. It's a nice day out."

"I'd like to show you something. Do you mind stepping away from your booth?" Noah coaxed.

"The beauty of this kind of market is that you hope things go missing."

The two seemingly un-relatable pairs walked toward the parking lot.

"There she is." Noah braced himself for judgment, but Marigold didn't seem surprised one bit.

"How long has she been like this?"

"Since I inherited her from my mother, and before that? Probably the 70s."

"I could paint her for you unless you brought me here for some other reason."

"I'd love you to paint her. I'm beginning to think that religion, politics, and money of all kinds were just supposed to be tools for society, like training wheels on a bicycle. But instead of learning how to balance and do cool tricks, without them, we've just put so many training wheels on that we are wobbling like crazy lunatics all over the path knocking into everyone and everything around us. Religion is the first training wheel I am taking off. I've decided believing in God and the Golden Rule is enough for me at the moment. Next, I'll work on removing the money training wheels. I doubt I will live long enough to see the political training wheels come off, but I guess I'm a hopeless romantic at any rate. If you can think it, it could happen, right?"

Marigold smiled.

"Noah. I know just how I will paint her up for you. I'll finish the bicycle, and we can swap rides till you come to visit me. Marigold tossed Noah his new keychain."

"Deal." Noah handed Marigold her's.

Vegan Cupcakes

After making their way back to the Free Market, Noah left Marigold, where he met her. Passing by the different free booths, something caught his eye: Books!!!

Walking over, he saw three people going through the stacks of books and magazines. Noah knew he didn't need more junk, but books were *never* junk. Book was an extension of himself. Books got Noah through his childhood and continued to get him through adulthood with grand stories and valuable information.

Books: A break away from the unfortunate reality of what was Noah's life.

There were about twenty-three seemingly random stacks of books on what looked like two twin-sized sheets laid side by side. No one appeared to be minding the stacks and Noah's mind immediately went to theft. It was taking him a while to mentally adjust to the idea that one could not steal what was free for the taking. There was no stress necessary surrounding security because, in essence, everything belonged to everyone at that moment.

Noah relaxed and browsed through, picking up anything that interested him. Then he stopped. Was *that* what he thought it was? A copy of "a book" stared him in the face, just lying there for the having. Noah didn't want to be greedy, so he waited to see if anyone else might be eyeing it. Nope. All three other people were deeply engrossed in their book or magazine of choice.

Noah grabbed it up, ran back to Marigold, and handed it to her with a quiet smile before jogging to where he left off, properly continuing his Free-Market adventure and feeling pretty good about himself. This was better than the church!

The Next sectioned-off area of stuff that interested him was a baker. This was amazing! Just to be sure, he checked for prices. None.

"Would yah like to try a vegan cupcake, darling?" A bright-eyed big-haired stereotypical Texan pushed a bright red cupcake with creamy icing practically up his nose.

"Do they taste any good?" Noah realized he sounded like a dick, but it was too late; no surprises there.

"Of course, they are! I made 'em sugar!" She shook her hair like Farrah Foset on a beach run.

Noah graciously accepted the vegan cupcake from the mental-model Texan and took a small bite after smelling it again carefully.

Noah's naivety led to his routinely expected lack of tact.

"Howdaya like it, cutie?" Her long black spider lashes were blinking wide in anticipation.

"Wow!" Noah was surprised. It was not only edible, but possibly the best cupcake he'd ever tasted. Noah wanted another one but decided this, of all things, would be rude. He lingered and looked at all the flavours and colours, and artwork.

"What's that?"

"Pistachio White Chocolate flavour! Here!" She practically shoved the cupcake up Noah's nostrils. Noah was delighted. But he was curious as usual and had to ask. For Noah, a question was just another itch to scratch. "Why vegan? What's wrong with animal products?"

"I wouldn't use the word "wrong." It's more that it's unnecessary. We don't need animal products to survive anymore. I believe nothing we get from animals is irreplaceable with the plant kingdom." She leaned forward and, for the first time since Noah first approached her booth, saw she was dead serious.

"I'm doing this to show folks that vegan can taste better and be better for the environment as well as for your body. I know they're cupcakes and all but ya gotta start somewhere, hun."

"What about all the farmers who would lose their jobs?" Noah pushed on.

"If people can retrain their brains to learn new things, People can retrain their brains to do something different for a living; going off animal products doesn't mean we go off needing farmers. Plus, that's assuming we will always need ways to exploit one another and our environment for our own selfish hunger." She paused and took a deep relaxing breath before continuing sweetly. "Darling, what about all the animals who live painful and short lives? Or get milked so much their tits get infected; puss and blood dripping shamelessly into the supply? Or all the hormones that get pumped in, or all the added sugar? Or how about all the baby animals being ripped from their mother's side after birth and disposed of accordingly? For what? For our insatiable hunger? A hunger that can be filled in less hateful, hurtful ways."

Noah argued passionately: "I love cheese!"

The bright-eyed, larger-than-life Texan popped open two chairs and ushered Noah to take a seat next to her before she went on: "I like torturing, killing, using, and abusing, but that doesn't make it right." The bubbly Texan looked Noah square in the eye as if locking him in place.

"Some farmers don't torture their animals; they treat them better than some humans get treated."

"And so, they should! But most don't, and when people use too much, demand goes too high for farmers and business people to justify the cost it takes to manage all the animals humanely. Not to mention all the water required, land needed, food, and travel costs, which all contribute to waste and carbon emissions. We worry about cars or breathing! Think of all those poor animals! Vegan food could taste much better than the alternative if we took the time to be creative and experiment."

Noah didn't like how much sense she was making, so he thanked her, accepted another cupcake, and told her he would think of the whole thing. Making no promises, he told her he'd try cutting down, but only because she and her cupcakes were so lovely.

One Strong Magnet

"We have a right to know. The information, history, and opinions we are being fed in our society don't match up with the rest of the world and what they are allowed to hear, say and write. It's time the bridge gap is closed and sealed up permanently between what is happening in our country, the world, and what we are being *told* is going on."

The man was sitting cross-legged on the grass. A crowd of fifty or sixty people has gathered around. Some seated for the whole thing, and some casually walked by after hearing something that may have caught their attention.

Right smack-dab front and centre, Noah saw his dog, Willie, relaxing with Yang under the shade of a tree. Noah crouched down and began shimmying his way through the welcoming and friendly group.

All the happy faces made him feel uncomfortable. The only smile that felt real was Yang's, mainly because he wasn't smiling. Noah had gotten so used to fake smiles and happiness in large groups that it all made him terribly uneasy.

The realness in a frown was worth a million fake upturned lips.

Then he realized why they were all smiling. These weren't fake smiles at all; they were stoner smiles. These people were relaxed and comfortable with themselves and the group. There was no hidden hostility, like in most places of worship, just acceptance, and love.

Noah let his guard part of the way down and took a proper seat. Prince William lazily moseyed over [practically crawling] to Noah, sleepily licking his lips before doing the same to Noah's hand. Then rolled back over onto his back between the two friends; the duty of greeting his human fulfilled.

Noah sat and listened for a few hours. He was in no rush. The longer he stayed, the less stuff he believed he would find to lug all the way back to his apartment. And after giving his old Jesus Wagon to Marigold, he needed a bit of faith in believing all of his stuff would be taken as well because he honestly had no idea how he would bring it back if it didn't all find new forever homes.

The man who was talking when Noah sat down got up and sat within the group. Then a woman got up and sat in his place.

She was heaven.

Noah was entranced immediately. Her hair was like a perfectly shaped black cotton ball with a daisy chain headband. Her skin was blacker than the night sky and her eyes shined like emeralds.

He didn't know her, but he loved her. Noah felt like he knew her from another lifetime but shook the uncomfortable thought from his mind.

"Hello, everyone." Her words sounded like a symphony of smiles. She had an accent, but Noah couldn't pinpoint exactly where from; it was like everywhere and nowhere, in particular, all at the same time.

"I go by the name Ash, but many of you know me simply as 'me.'"

Noah's puzzled look shifted to Yang as he took the joint from his left hand.

Yang's Cheshire grin said it all, but to remove all doubt, he mouthed the word clearly to Noah, "*surprise!*"

Noah watched every move, from her expressive eyebrows to her bare toes wiggling in the grass, soaking up the textures.

"I wrote a book. Well, sort of. It's more like a manual for my ideal world. I wrote it because I had to. It wrote itself, and it has been writing itself since I was a small child." Her eyes sparkled.

"Most of my ideas came from other people, other places. Some I have known about since I was little and didn't know where I got the ideas or why they stuck in my memories so strongly. Other ideas are fairly recent, either from people telling me about them or me sitting in my head for days, weeks, months, or even years at a time. In a way, this book was written by everyone. I hope that makes sense."

Her eyes met Noah's and locked. She was not afraid.

"I examined everything and everyone. I always have. I am hyper-sensitive, and I overthink the smallest things. I have to understand. Things have to make sense and be fair; otherwise, I won't let go." Her eyes unlocked and moved intently around the group.

"There were loads of things that didn't make sense to me growing up; loads of unfair circumstances. I kept asking *why*. Why would a God or, indeed, a leader or ruler for the people promote such things? I grew older, apathetic, and just wanted

to die. I made a number of horrible choices and prayed to a God, and God would take me away from all this mess."

Noah connected. She was no longer beautiful. She was him. He was she. They were one and the same yet completely different.

"I had always written my feelings and thoughts on things; writing solutions seemed to be the only way my heart and mind would allow me to let things go. But it wasn't until my darkest hours that I started to put these bits of writing together. My family stepped in at one point and pulled me out by force from the personal hell I had condemned myself to. I was too tired to kick and scream, so I expressed hatred, frustration, and blame. Why would they bring me into this world? And why would they force me *back* into this world that kicked them while they were down just as much as it kicked me?"

Ash was captivating, clear-spoken, peaceful, and strong. The crowd grew and silenced themselves, and Noah barely noticed.

"When I began socializing again, it was like the first time. When I began making choices again, it was like the first time. I look back in amazement at how much can be stripped from a being when, like me, you give up and stop climbing toward your ideals. When you think your life is pointless or that you don't deserve to be loved and respected like all living beings, this is when the negativity takes a seat in your soul and drives you to apathetic self-loathing."

A small boy, about thirteen years old, spoke:

"How do you stop the hurting?"

She smiled lovingly at the almond-eyed youth: "You don't."

She leaned forward in his direction, "I grew up in Ireland, and in Ireland, we have trains that run on lines. One day I was on the train headed to Dublin. If I was late to school, I didn't get a seat, so it was important to get on the train. This train on this particular morning was packed with no available seats and loads of people needing to get somewhere to do something just like me, and equally important, I would imagine. But there was this truck, and it had destroyed part of the line's track, so the train had to stop halfway into town. Some people got off in search of another way there, others got angry or started cracking jokes as the conductors worked to solve the problem, and I just sat and waited. Eventually, the line was fixed, and I had a seat the rest of the way into town with plenty of leg room!" She chuckled.

"The train is you. The track is your path. The truck is all the hurt and obstacles you face. All the people on board represent all the different ways you can handle or look at the situation in order to get through your trials. Sometimes we are impatient and hop off our path to take a longer route just to get to the same place and pay the same or greater price. Sometimes we hop off and beat the crowd. Sometimes we stay and get angry or distract ourselves as best we can, and then sometimes, we manage to sit and ride it out patiently until we are able to continue on our path. Who is to say one way is better than the next? Only you. Life throws us wobblers constantly. Just when you think you have it sorted, another wobbler. I was told what doesn't kill you makes you stronger. So, I guess the answer to our question revolves around how you choose to deal with things. If you are hurting because of an obstacle or an unexpected, unfortunate event, do you decide to allow it to throw you off your own train and hope it all goes in your favour? Do

you distract yourself or sink into your hurt and negativity? Or do you stay clear-headed, sit, and mentally prepare yourself for the rest of the journey? It's entirely up to you. I've tried all versions. The funniest part about it is that I'm still headed toward my desired destination. I am just enjoying it now."

She released the young man from her focus at that moment; knowing he understood and sat up straight to shift her attention back to the group: "This book was my way of trying to fix the train tracks for future travellers, so maybe your pain and anguish wouldn't be as bad as mine was. My thought was that maybe if I offered solutions to problems I saw, others would be able to act on them. Maybe if my book offered one solution to one person's problem, maybe things might get a little easier for us all. The truth is, I have no idea how to stop the hurting other than feel it fully, learn as much as I can from it, and then, most importantly: move forward from it. Remember: Don't get stuck in the pain or the lesson so much that you forget to move forward."

She smiled sweetly again before continuing, "I am fumbling in the dark just as much as the rest of the world. But I do know things could be happier, healthier, cleaner, and more peaceful for us all. And if we all did little bits to change ourselves here and there, then there would be no reason we couldn't make all that stuff happen."

The boy asked another question:

"Am I valuable?"

"To the rest of the Universe? No. Neither am I. But it feels good to think we are. I guess it keeps us waking up each morning and playing the game."

The boy continued to push:

"Then why am I here?"

"Why are any of us here? I can't answer these questions for you. I can only answer that for myself. I have decided I'm here to be the best example I can be. I'm here to improve myself. I'm here to humble myself. I'm here to smell the tulips. I'm here to learn from my mistakes and unhelpful choices. I'm here to be kind and to love even when it hurts. I am here to forgive. Why are you here?"

Everyone was silent.

The boy answered:

"I am here to ask questions."

Everyone listening began to laugh themselves to tears.

Another man spoke up:

"A lot of the stuff you write about isn't new."

"Yes. Sir, you are correct. All of my ideas are not my own. Even my language was taught to me. The only thing I did was put it all together in a way that makes sense to me, the way you see it. I went to a Free-Market years ago, and they hold a special place in my heart. Forgiveness meetings, well, I didn't invent forgiveness, and I didn't invent meetings. All I did was put them together. That is why the author is 'me,' because when you read the book, the author is *you*. The way you read, understand, and use what you read makes all of you the authors."

The man chuffed:

"I didn't write it. You did."

"I didn't set up this Free-Market; WE did," Ash replied.

The man kept on making a point:

"I didn't set it up."

"Are you here?"

The man looked around at everyone, chuckling:

"Yeah. Pretty sure. But I didn't organize it."

"If all of you weren't here, would there even be a Free-Market right now?" The man was silent. She continued, "Probably not a very good one, right? Same with 'a book,' it is just words on a page until you read it and breathe life into it. You know that sort of way?"

She had the sweetest smile, Noah thought

In typically "Noah" fashion, words poured out, skipping all social filters, "This seems beneath you. How did you find us? Why aren't you charging for this?"

"I was called, and I accepted the invitation, and I came to meet someone I owe a favour and a great deal of appreciation to."

"Who?"

"Besides all of you? A man named Hank."

"Why?"

"Because my heart tells me to. There is more to him than what greets you on the surface, like with all of us to some extent." Noah's excitement and openness shrivelled into pain-filled jeal-

ousy. But he loved his friend like a brother, so it didn't last as long as he hoped it would.

His curiousness and the expression on his face told her this man not only knew who Hank was but where she could find him. But instead of asking and pushing, she patiently waited.

Noah understood exactly what she was doing, and even though he wanted her for his own, he wanted her happiness more. So, he answered her telepathic question softly.

"He is playing Mahjong."

Noah's balloon heart deflated.

Ash readdressed the crowd and thanked them for their time. Noah volunteered to walk her over with Yang to meet Hank, mainly to spend more time with her. She had a healing, protective presence he had never felt before. It was as though the ideal was not only possible but expected when she was around. Her strong, peaceful confidence put him at ease, and all his confusion and pessimistic thoughts fell to the ground like robes that were way too big to fit.

When she spoke to people and touched them as they slowly walked around the Free Market, Noah could see their internal pains melt away. Relief.

The feelings of love and understanding were so strong that Noah's eyes couldn't help but release the feelings in the form of tears, and they burned.

They had acquired a following by the time they reached the Mahjong table. Wherever she went, whatever booth she visited became busy within minutes of her presence.

Yang pointed it out to Noah, but Noah couldn't explain it, so he dismissed the possibility altogether.

Yang persisted, "Noah. She is like a positive magnet. Attracting opposites. Stronger the magnet, the stronger the attraction. You see?"

"Okay, Yang." It made Noah uncomfortable. "You trying to say we are all negative, Yang?"

"Nope, just saying she is one strong magnet."

PERFECTION PERSPECTIVE

Hank and Tommy had three tables of Mahjong going. Children, adults, and seniors are all mixed up based on ability.

Hank saw Ash walking toward him. Time stopped.

"Are you Hank?"

"One of the many."

"I brought you something." Riffling through her bag, she carefully pulled out 'a book' and handed it to Hank.

"I'm no architect." She shyly smiled.

He opened the cover and a pop-up paper cut out of a house stared him straight in the eye.

"Sorry. That's my best version. I was worried it would offend you, but then I did it anyway."

Hank laughed, "I love it! Did Annie and Allie help?"

"No. But they loved the gifts. They made you cards to thank you." She pulled out two different coloured envelopes covered in stickers and glitter.

Noah was surprised at how close they were.

"Uh, Hank, how do you know her?"

"Ali helped. I've been skyping her with Ahmed for the last few weeks. We all wanted to surprise you. Surprise!"

"Who are Annie and Allie?"

"My daughters."

Noah turned to Ash, "How old are you?"

"Never ask a woman her age Noah, geese pal!"

"It's okay, Hank. Noah, I am thirty-seven."

"Are you married?" Noah pressed on as Hank rolled his eyes and then threw his head back in discomfort and disappointment. Ash was unphased by Noah's twenty-one questions.

"Separated. Ireland is progressive only when it wants to be and is a bit behind in everything else, so it takes a while to divorce. Unfortunately, my wife is very angry, but she won't talk to anyone, counselling has only recently started to become more socially acceptable, but it still isn't near what it should be. I tried sticking by her, but her anger led to violence, and when I realized she was blacking out in rage, I started to really fear for myself and our girls. The cheating, the lying, and everything else; I just dealt with it the good old-fashioned Irish way: I stuck it out.

She asked me for a separation after I lost my job and took all our money out of our mutual bank account. Long story short, it has been almost four years. And I'm getting nervous."

"Where are your girls now?"

Noah's nosiness knew no bounds; Yang was now rolling his eyes in silent protest.

"They are with her. Our social system ruled in her favour. After she took all our savings, told me she had been cheating

on me since we met, and demanded separation, I was left with nothing. I fought for them and am still fighting for them, but she has better solicitors, and the health services don't want to separate them from their biological mother. My eggs, her body. But she was the pregnant one and had more monies. I go to court and call HSE, but she tells lies and stories and puts on a good face. The girls are too scared of her to question her authority.

Plus, she looks more Irish than me even though I'm born Irish, and she was adopted from another country."

"Why don't you take them?"

"Stop, Noah. This is personal." *Yang's Polite-o-meter was steaming red.*

"He is fine, Yang; I have nothing to hide. It's because the only way I can change the laws to help future generations is to follow them, so I have a legal voice. Doesn't matter if the laws are unjust, illogical, or unfair. Hank has helped me form my arguments for court over the last few weeks. It doesn't hurt that she seems more interested in the money than she is in my girls, so I have more power than I thought."

"Hank?" Noah's focus switched from her to Hank, who just shrugged off the good deed as though it was a social obligation, not something worthy of any praise.

Ash came right up to Hank and embraced him with so much feeling.

Noah watched the hard-as-nails Hank turn into a giant furry teddy bear. Jealousy found itself in Noah's heart again, but this time with her ability to connect so deeply with Hank.

"Noah, I told Ash she could stay with us. I couldn't ask you because it was a surprise. I figured you could pick her brain over a long game of Mahjong. I might even have a coffee."

Noah walked over to Hank in a panic and whispered in his ear, "Hank! She can't see all my clutter. We can't just leave all my shit in the park!"

"Who's to say it's all there? Besides, I'd be more bothered by your rolling billboard."

"I traded it for a bicycle today. Marigold has no idea I am giving it to her, but that is beside the point."

Dumbfounded, Hank shook Noah by the shoulders, "Wow! Hey! I am proud of you, pal! Great news!"

"Thanks. But that doesn't solve the stuff problem."

"Before you go gettin' your panties twisted, go check it out and see what's left."

Noah couldn't argue with him there, so he swiftly walked in the direction of his stuff to assess the possible damages.

He walked so quickly that he got to Marigold's art stand and had to turn around; he went too far. So, with a quick wave, he awkwardly jogged back in search of his pile of baggage.

"Hey, Noah. Where are you going, friend?" Ahmed was sitting in the refurbished beach chair right where Noah left him much earlier in the day.

Noah has so turned around that he looked all over for his piles, but they were all gone. How could that be? "Where is all my stuff, Ahmed?"

"It has been Free Cycled, my friend! Noah sat next to Ahmed, checking out what was left."

"No one liked my records?"

"Everyone liked them."

"So why are they still here?"

"Because someone fixed your record player, so I decided to keep these for you. Good idea, yes?"

"Nice! How did you manage that one?"

"I didn't. A man you gave suits came back when you were gone and fixed your player."

"Who took the rest of it?"

"Many people. It was a very cleansing experience for me. I kept thinking of my mother. She would have loved this. I secretly pretended I gave all her things instead. When the last thing left, I could feel such release. No more shame or guilt. Just peace."

"Thank you for helping me today. I don't think I could have done that." Noah was humbled.

"No, No. Thank *you*, brother."

Noah sighed a deep relief; *this was happiness.*

FULL CIRCLE CYCLE

It was an amazing experience. Ahmed and Ali took Yang, Hank, Ash, the record player, and records to their respective homes for the evening. Noah insisted on riding his artwork back with the tired pooch in his very own bicycle basket. Marigold was kind to give Noah a blanket for the little fella, and within minutes the prince had properly passed the fuck out from exhaustion.

Halfway home, Noah stopped by the fountain in the centre of the town and lit the congratulatory joint Yang had rolled for him in honour of his big day. It was 11:23 at night, so the small town was pretty much dead. Closing his eyes, taking a deep breath, and raising his arms in the air, Noah felt free. It was right then, on the exhale, that he decided adamantly he would never get in his own way again. Two seconds later, he heard a familiar voice:

"Hello, sir!"

William woke up from his basket of sleep startled and ready to fight.

"Woah! There is the mighty one! I brought you your favourite meat stick!"

The Older Gentleman always seemed to get a kick out of saying dirty things within the context of a clean conversation.

Noah adjusted his eyes to the darkness and saw the Dapper-Dressed Older Gentleman from the bookshop.

"Hello. Sorry for the smoking; I am sort of celebrating. Haven't seen you in a long time. How's the bookshop?"

"Busy as any bookshop in a digital age, but I stay optimistic." Then eyeing the fatty rolled in Noah's left fingers to perfection, "And no apologies needed if you are willing to share, young man. In my day, the rule was puff-puff-pass, but you younger folks tend to do things differently these days, I guess."

Noah couldn't believe it! Did everyone smoke cannabis? Was this some sort of secret club where you only meet fellow stoners' mid-toke?

Too shocked to say anything but wanting the Older Gentleman to know he heard him, he ceremoniously puff-puff then passed.

The Older Gentleman inhaled with such lung strength a quarter of the joint was gone! No cough! Noah was clearly impressed.

"So, young man. What are we celebrating?" By this time, Prince William was wrapped in his new blanket and already curled up on the Older Gentleman's lap.

"Well, a lot of things in my life have changed since you handed me that book."

No response.

"I read half of it so far, which inspired me to start the Personal Steps. I met a houseless man named Hank at my first Forgiveness Meeting and moved him into my apartment with me. I quit my job, got a new job, picked up a pot as a temporary crutch and healthier alternative to stress, and gave away ninety per-

cent of my stuff at a Free Market that was held in my honour today."

Noah paused to reflect kindly. "That must sound crazy."

Passing Noah the half-smoked joint, the Older Gentleman showed no emotion as he spoke on the exhale, "Nope. Not really."

Trying at this point to get a reaction, Noah just started throwing random bits out:

"I met the author of 'a book' today at the Free Market."

Nothing.

"She is staying with Hank and me at my de-cluttered apartment tonight."

Again, nothing.

"I got rid of my Jesus wagon and traded it for this sweet new ride."

"I like the bike. Good trade. Ash is lovely. Ask her about the next steps."

"Which steps?" Noah forgot.

"The Family steps. I thought you read half the book already?"

"I did; I just forgot, that's all. A lot has happened since then."

"Well, before she leaves, ask her about the Family steps. She always leaves before you want her to, and when she leaves, she is very hard to get a hold of again. Don't take my word for it. Anyway, she is a wealth of experience and understanding, so

if I were you, I couldn't be anywhere that she isn't while she is around. You get me?"

The Older Gentleman thanked Noah for the company, got up, put the prince back in his bicycle basket, and walked off into the night.

Looking around, Noah finished his first celebratory joint, hopped on his bicycle, and cycled back to the apartment as fast as he could.

He was slow, but he was getting there.

The idea of doing the Family Steps petrified him, but the nice thing about Noah being stoned and on a mission was that not even fear could stop him.

He liked his ability to think clearly when he was stoned. He liked who he was without stress. So much so that the idea of doing other drugs didn't interest him but growing a plant or two was sounding better and better. Cheap, clean, organic. No thugs, no dirty money, no pills, and no nonsense. He would discuss it with Yang the next time he saw him.

A clean, green cycling machine, Noah remembered the first lonely drive home from that church meeting; thoughts of death and suicide.

Death no longer bothered him the way it used to. Nor did he crave its arrival. Noah was happy and at peace, so much so that he decided at that moment when he did finally die that was exactly how he wanted to feel: happy and at peace.

As he approached the candle-lit apartment and carried the bike up the steps, Noah wondered if there was anything about his life that had not changed besides his wardrobe.

He turned the handle, and he knew he didn't care.

Noah loved who he was and who he was becoming. After forgiving himself, Changing Uncomfortably, and Free-Cycling most of his possessions away, Noah had properly deconstructed as best he could.

Mistakes, misjudgements, mishaps, and mayhem; He was ready for his next few steps.

As he entered the apartment, he could feel the warmth and love; Noah was finally home, and this was His Family.

The End...

Until Book 2: Love your history, be open to change and when in doubt, forgive.

CPSIA information can be obtained
at www.ICGtesting.com
Printed in the USA
BVHW042243131122
651666BV00051B/985/J